Paul Wenz (1869-1939) arrived in Australia in 1892 and worked as a grazier on the property 'Nanima' in the Forbes district from 1898, where he wrote several popular novels and many short stories of Australian bush life. These were published in Paris. His only work published in English was *Diary of a New Chum* in 1908 (ETT Imprint 1990), an edition that also contains his correspondence with André Gide and Miles Franklin. His novel *The Thorn in the Flesh* (ETT Imprint 2004) was translated by Maurice Blackman and introduced by Helen Garner. Wenz died in Australia in 1939.

Marie Ramsland, BA, MLitt, PhD, *Chevalier des Palmes Académiques*, is a conjoint lecturer at the University of Newcastle, Australia. Her main research interests are French/Australian literary & cultural connections and translation, with recent articles on the Great War. In 2016, her book entitled *Restless Sojourner in France* was published. It details the French translations of the novels of Australian author Dymphna Cusack. Marie's translations from French include *Hanoi Blues* by Jeanne Cordelier and *The Culverin* by Michel Tournier.

*Paul and Hettie Wenz at Cannes 1918, before returning home
to Australia (courtesy Nicole Wenz)*

THEIR FATHERS' LAND: FOR KING AND EMPIRE

Novel & Short Stories by

PAUL WENZ

Introduced & translated by Marie Ramsland

ETT IMPRINT
Exile Bay

Publisher's Dedication
to Jean-Paul Delamotte

First published in 2018 by ETT Imprint, Exile Bay

Translation and Introduction © Marie Ramsland 2018

ETT IMPRINT
PO Box R1906
Royal Exchange NSW 1225
Australia

ISBN 978-1-925706-46-8 (paper)
ISBN 978-1-925706-47-5 (ebook)

Design by Hanna Gotlieb

CONTENTS

INTRODUCTION

Paul Wenz, French-Australian writer:
'en contact direct avec la beauté de la nature et à la
noblesse humaine'

Born in Reims on 18 August 1869 into a wealthy and enterprising Protestant family of German descent, Paul Wenz soon found that he had no aptitude or interest in joining the family's prosperous wool firm, Wenz & Co, asserting: 'I was no good to the Firm, and the Firm was no good to to me!' He had, nevertheless, worked there for three months in a clerical position, but a record of his time there 'is practically empty'.[1] Paul claimed that he 'withered like a climbing plant in a basket. I needed air. The business invited me to get some'. He was sent across the Channel to London – a city he found *'étonnant et mystérieux* [astonishing and mysterious]' – for nine months specifically to learn English. Then he went to Algeria to study viticulture. His parents considered him 'whimsical, curious and unpredictable', with an outlook on life different from his brothers and sister. He much preferred the outdoor life, adventure and travel that led him to settle permanently, with his father's eventual agreement and support, on the other side of the globe, in Australia, raising sheep, inventing farming equipment, writing and travelling the world – regularly visiting France to see his family. He had

had the privilege of travelling the world before permanently settling in Australia. His father had considered this a necessary part of his sons' education.

In Reims, Paul started school in the Catholic system remaining there until the final years of high school when he claims to have lost two years of his youth being fed poorly, both intellectually and physically. 'Fortunately, my family noticed in time that the *lycée* hardly suited me; I was sent to Paris to an independent school'.[2] The Ecole Alsacienne opened in 1871 in the *rue des Ecoles*, Paris, before moving to 109, *rue Notre Dame-Des-Champs* in the 6th arrondissement on the left bank of the Seine, was begun by Protestant teachers from Strasbourg in Alsace who wanted to be French nationals. Its students, many as boarders, came mainly from wealthy elite families. The main aim of this laic institution, which was recognised by the French Government, was to produce cultured men and humanists.

A general broad-based curriculum, taught by friendly mentoring teachers, included history, geography, Ancient Greek, Latin, physics, chemistry and Natural History. Emphasis on French language and literature, foreign languages, theatre, art, music and sport was designed so that each student would reach their potential. While Paul was a mediocre student, he was popular with the other students. He spent nine years in Paris, returning home for holidays and spending some weekends with schoolmates. In the senior years when he had free time, he would spend days, and most evenings in summer, in the Jardin du Luxembourg. Paul spoke about the lessons different from his earlier schooling as they were '*intéressantes et souvent même amusantes* [interesting and often even amusing]'. Paul emphasised lessons he had for music, dance, deportment and horse-riding.[3]

It was on one of his return voyages from France to Australia in 1896 that Paul met Harriet (Hettie) Adela Annette Dunn, a daughter of a well-established Australian grazier. Paul was already living in a small cottage on Nanima Station – on Wiradjeri Aboriginal land on the banks of the Lachlan River near Forbes in the central west of New South Wales – and negotiating to purchase the property. The couple married in September1898 and moved into a newly-constructed homestead.

Here (in the homestead on the steep banks of the Lachlan) Paul wrote his stories, helped in English translation by Hettie's remarkable knowledge of French and English, at times even more exact than his own. Here, they read and never lacked entertainment – in a library that grew to comprise over 200 thousand volumes.[4]

Not long after returning from the usual, typically long overseas trip, Paul fell ill with pneumonia in July 1939. He died in the Crombic Private Hospital, Forbes, on 23 August just after his seventieth birthday. He had crossed the world, sailed every ocean, visited the Americas, Asia and Oceania. Hettie moved to live in the Pacific Hotel in the sea and harbourside suburb of Manly, Sydney. She died twenty years later and is buried with her husband in the Forbes cemetery.[5] They had visited many countries which they found 'ceaselessly fascinating, beguilingly new'.

From Australia, they travelled all over the Pacific, around Cape Horn and through the Magellan Straits, through the Panama Canal and around South Africa. They took the Trans-Siberian train from Vladivostok through Russia, before the revolution and penetrated into parts of Asia never before seen by white man or woman.

The lure of the jungle and desert, danger and distance drew them to Rhodesia, the Victoria Falls, Morocco and the centre of Africa, South America and far up the Amazon River ...[6]

Several of Wenz's short stories, published and unpublished, reveal Paul's fascination with the countries they visited, especially several he wrote for his young nephews and nieces. (He and Hettie had no children of their own.) These resemble traditional fairy tales (*contes de fée*) and it is clear that Paul had been influenced by the writings of both seventeenth-century French author Charles Perrault and the nineteenth-century German brothers Jacob and Wilhelm Grimm. Paul's stories, often

7

set in exotic countries, include *L'Eléphant et la tomate* (The Elephant and the Tomato); *La Petite sirène* (The Young Mermaid); *La Maison dans la forêt* (The House in the Forest); *La Clef d'or* (The Golden Key); *L'Eméraude* (The Emerald); *Le Bon pirate* (The Good Pirate). Others reveal Wenz's understanding of different cultures he encountered during his many travels and many are heavily auto-fictional, especially those set in Australia.

Before settling permanently in Australia, Paul had spent two years jackarooing on properties in Victoria and New South Wales providing him with valuable rural experiences he was able to use in his writings. Also crucial for his portrayal of Australian life were the works of the early "bush" writers – such as Henry Kendall, Henry Lawson and Banjo Paterson. These writers promoted the pioneering ethics, held by their ancestors as Australia's first "immigrants", of striving to establish a new nation that reproduced, but at the same time modified, where they had come from and thus ensured prosperity for future generations. As well, they introduced ideas of egalitarianism and mateship amongst the people living on the land. These qualities were used to define the Australian soldier in the wars fought for King and Empire particularly the South African War and World War I.[7]

Paul used the pseudonym Paul Warrego – from the Warrego River which runs from southwest Queensland into the Darling River in central northern New South Wales – for his first book published as *A l'autre bout du monde. Aventures et mœurs Australiennes* comprising sixteen stories – all but five are set in Australia.[8] His second collection of stories appeared in 1911, *Sous la Croix du Sud. Contes Australiens* with ten of the twelve stories revealing the ups and downs of country life.[9] Life in the outback preoccupied Wenz throughout his literary output. His *Diary of a New Chum* – the only book he wrote in English – contains impressions of the bush with autobiographical elements and anecdotes and is 'rich in curious details of social history'.[10] The concept of the "new chum" is a familiar stereotype in Australian literature and popular cinema, especially comedy: often an educated man from Britain who is able to view bush life as an outsider while absorbing what is Australian and Australia.[11] The "new chum" appears in several of Wenz's stories.

He is able to evoke both the beauty and the harshness of the land-scape in parallel with the ambiguity of living in the outback. His char-acters – depicted realistically using humour, irony, pathos, violence, poignancy and sentiment, like Lawson, Paterson and other popular writers of the time – include jackaroos, swagmen, rabbiters, boundary riders, wagoners, miners, publicans, shearers, workers, farmers, gra-ziers, station bosses and owners, storekeepers, women and children. The protagonists are practical and often show a philosophical outlook on life: 'Man cannot create without torturing or destroying', accord-ing to Wenz.[12]

Throughout his writings Wenz uses typical themes, settings, inci-dents and characters, so it is no surprise that an early published novel *L'Homme du soleil couchant* (The Sundowner, 1923) is set in the gold- ields with a rapidly-developing town, initiated by a "new chum", followed by its decline and then its reconstruction. The author dedi-cated the book to his wife Hettie: '... *une Australienne qui m'a fait comprendre et aimer l'Australie* [an Australian woman who made me understand and love Australia] ...'. The novel is remarkable for the descriptions of Australian outback landscapes, goldmining methods and equipment, the construction and expansion of a town with its many public houses (pubs), dwelling huts, school and so on. Wenz vividly depicts the inhabitants of the town, including its children and their informal and formal education.

The manuscript of the novel, started in 1911, had been taken to France when Hettie and Paul set off on one of their long travels. It became serialised in the popular literary magazine *La Revue de Paris* in 1915. Several short stories depicting the impact of the First World War were written by Wenz while working for the wartime Red Cross in Reims (1914-1915) and in London (1916-19). These appeared in 1919 in two collections published by Berger-Levrault: *Bonnes gens de la Grande Guerre* and *Choses d'hier*. Also inspired by the events of the Great War, the manuscript of Wenz's novel *Le Pays de leurs pères* was sent to the *Revue de Paris* and was serialised in 1918 before being republished in book form the following year by Calmann-Lévy with the dedication to those 'who crossed the seas to get [themselves] messed up':

AUX HOMMES
QUI SONT VENUS D'AUSTRALIE ET DE LA
NOUVELLE ZELANDE
POUR SE BATTRE AVEC NOUS

A LA MEMOIRE
DE CEUX QUE GARDERA NOTRE TERRE DE FRANCE
P. W.[13]

The socially, ever-active couple returned to their sheep property in November that year after nearly six years absence. During that time, Paul had kept in touch with the manager of his property Walter Gow and some of these letters were passed on to the press

During the long war years, Paul and Hettie worked tirelessly to ameliorate the impact of war. At first, Paul delivered various material and medical supplies and food for hospitals in the countryside around Reims and transported the wounded in his black-and-yellow Hotchkiss vehicle, which he lovingly called "The Wasp", to the nearest railway station as the German invaders approached 'the ancient city where the kings of France had come to be crowned, where ... Joan of Arc had stood in 1429'. The initial attack on the city lasted thirteen days wreaking death and destruction, causing intense fear and significant damage to the famous Notre-Dame Cathedral which was being used as a hospital:

Paul: ... The shells have started a big fire somewhere – and it's spreading quickly.

Hettie: You're right Paul... Dear Heavens! It's the Cathedral!

Paul: *Mon Dieu*! And the German prisoners are there! I must hurry!

Effects: Running Feet, Shouts, Crackle of Flames

Paul: You there, help me! There are men in the Cathedral! We must get them out. The roof is on fire.

1st Voice: I don't risk my life for the Boche, mon ami. Let them stay there and fry in their own fire!

Paul: Boche or not, they're human beings...

2nd Voice: Not me Monsieur. The German swine can die! Look at our Cathedral! The stained glass windows are broken already and they are irreplaceable! Damn the Boche!

Paul: There's no time to argue, and we can't let men burn to their death in there ...

Narrator: Paul and a few other civilians brought the German prisoners to safety ... In the strife-filled years that followed, he risked his life many times, conveying cases of material for hospitals between England and France – on a channel where the sign of the Red Cross did not ensure protection.[14]

In his autobiography, Paul spoke of seeing his primary school, L'Enfant Jésus, for the first time in 1914 after leaving thirty-seven years earlier. It was also being used as a hospital. Sister Sainte Algaé, who had taught him, was now a nurse. 'I stood before her without saying my name. She looked me straight in the eye for a brief moment and, without hesitating, she said my name. She had hardly changed. She had the same chubby face of a healthy peasant, made for the outdoors rather than the cloister'.[15]

The family home and the Wenz work offices suffered damage from the constant intense bombardment on the city. They took refuge, like many others, in underground cellars where work continued for as long as possible.[16] October 1916 brought the family news of the death of Jean Wenz, Paul's nephew. Jean, who had spent two years in Australia, was serving as an interpreter for the 3rd Infantry Australian Brigade Head-quarters during the Battle of the Somme.

Earlier in March 1916, Paul was transferred to London as liaison officer with the French Committee of the Red Cross. 'My new duties [later described as 'quietly carrying out our humble and hardly glorious tasks'] change me into what I never wanted ..., an office man. But this war is good for us as it forces us to accept every kind of sacrifice'. Hettie was busy preparing comfort parcels for French soldiers (*poilus*) with things sent from Australia. They often included letters – some for French children.[17] She also worked in an Australian canteen. Paul became familiar with the sight-impaired patients at St Dunstan's Hospital in London's Regent Park. The hospital had been established by Sir Arthur Pearson (blind himself) in the home of Otto Kahn, an American banker, in 1915 especially for servicemen blinded in the war. They were transferred from the 2nd London General Hospital (begun in mid-1914) in St Mark's College, Chelsea, where they had been cared for along with other wounded men who:

> arrived in a deplorable condition – haggard, dirty with matted hair, unshaven, and their clothes stiff with mud and blood from wounds. Most had wounds of the upper extremities, nearly all due to shrapnel rather than rifle bullets ... most of the wounds were septic by the time they reached the Hospital ... Some soldiers were suffering from rheumatism and sciatica, attributed by them to being constantly in wet trenches.[18]

St Dunstan's had a specialised rehabilitation and education program. By the end of the war, over 600 veterans had been trained in various occupations, such as remedial massage, typing, poultry farming, carpentry, basket and mat making and shoe and boot repairing; 700 were being trained for new occupations and 200 were still in rehabilitation.[19]

The Wenzes' '*petit* [small] flat' was conveniently only two miles from the hospital:

> We are regulars at this establishment and I rarely miss going to see them dance on Friday evenings. The blind Australians often come to our place for dinner and we are happy to do something for them. This contact with the blind Australians ... suggested *Le Pays de leurs pères* that the *Revue de Paris* has accepted, and which will come out in a few months time.[20]

A reviewer for *Illustration* pointed out the close connection between this novel and the author's earlier "bush" stories with their descriptions of early immigrant settlers who established their new home in the harsh, isolated Australian outback where 'birth, life and death are reduced to their simplest form'. The younger generation responded enthusiastically to the call-to-arms from Britain brought to the outback verbally by the mailman and by delivering metropolitan newspapers containing war propaganda. Jim and Dick joined 2,500 men aboard a transport ship heading for Gallipoli and the Western Front. They are both wounded on the Front and wake up in neighbouring beds in a London hospital. As they slowly recover, they take pleasure in discovering their forebears' country. A paragraph extract, taken from the *British Australasian* newspaper, appeared in the *Sydney Stock and Station Journal* of early January 1919. It referred to the acceptance for publication of *Le Pays de leurs pères* that: 'concerns itself with the doings of our boys whom M[onsieur] Wenz knows and loves so well, in the present war. It will be sure to interest all A.I.F. men who can read French, and later I hope there will be an English translation'.[21] And many years later, here it is.

The writing is instinctively seductive, devoid of convention and banality.[22] The characters are well drawn and contrasts between England and Australia are highlighted within the narrative. To emphasise the authenticity of his stories, Wenz used actual names of places, properties, towns, geographical features, newspaper and magazine titles and so on, without resorting to a French equivalent. Examples include: *Tin Pot Creek*; *Lone Man Plain*; *Back Paddock*; beer *Imperial*; *Bluegum Hole*; *Harbour*; *"heads"* [entry to Sydney harbour]; *Bulletin*; *Taratoola Chronicle*. These were usually italicised. Names of native birds, animals and plants are either apostrophised or italicised, sometimes both – like "myall"; "salt bush"; "cotton bush"; *"bull dog"* [ants]; *roo*; *mopoke*; *curlew* – some are footnoted in French, like *galahs** perruches and *swagmen** chemineaux. Italics were also used for emphasis. The author sought to inject specific Australian words and expressions in his writings to evoke aspects of Australian culture that he was personally familiar with. English expressions in dialogue conveyed affection, intimacy and mateship – often enhanced by humour: *Bless you, miss*; *good old Sam*; *All right, my dear boy*; *Good evening*; *Three cheers for England.*

Several expressions were used on purpose not only for convenience, but to remind the reader that the story concerned Australian life and Australians, even when a French equivalent would have sufficed: squatter; convict; bush; selector; at home; mailman; parson; spear; skating rink; University man; storekeeper; boss; policeman; stockwhip; teacher; stewardess; nurse; girl; tailor made; anthem. These are but a few examples. Words specific to the Australian and British culture include *billy*; *cricketer*; *cooee*; *pickles*; *homestead*; *boundary rider*; *stockman* and *rouseabout*. Temperature, height, weight and currency were conveyed according to Australian usage with the French equivalent also given for the targeted reading public. Nicknames and abbreviations in English enhanced the "Australianness" of the story, such as "Frilly"; "doc"; *Maggie*; *joe* [Joey]; *stumpy*; *wingy*.

Thirteen short stories about the war – semi-autobiographical, semi-documentary with careful attention to authenticity and at times highly romanticised – vividly depict the situation from the outset in

Reims and the outlying areas under attack by the German army. Painterly, poetic descriptive or contextual passages, they confront the reader directly with everyday activities and the naked emotions of both citizens and soldiers. While the author doesn't shirk from forcefully depicting the ravages of war, he emphasises positive qualities of that experience, often with a touch of humour, such as courage, bravery, persistence, self-sacrifice, respect for life, leadership and mateship, or camaraderie.

In *Bonnes gens de la Grande Guerre*, we read of a wounded Irishman being cared for in the Trianon Palace at Versailles that had been transformed into an English army hospital. The bed next to his was occupied by a severely disfigured German soldier; the wounded were visited by English officers and Frenchwomen. Recovered sufficiently to be allowed to leave the hospital for a few hours each day, Patrick gets acquainted with the city and the people and is helped by a well-build sapper of the French army and a friendship begins and intensifies – an *entente cordiale* (like the original understanding established between Britain and France in 1904). A squad of twenty-one soldiers, including Patrick, were to leave Versailles on a four-day recreation leave to England before returning to the Front. So the two friends spend the final hours before they are to be separated talking and drinking. When the roll call is taken as the men board the train at the Versailles-Chantiers station, Pat Nolan 4702 is missing. He turns up at the hospital the following day, disorientated and confused, wearing an oversized kepi and greatcoat, is locked up where he tries to reconstruct what happened …

In "Le Rachat d'Etienne Muffot" (Etienne Muffot's Redemption), the protagonist decides to hide his transport vehicle from the Germans and goes fishing. He returns after hearing explosions in the city to find his home in ruins. He then seeks refuge like others in the cellars where he enjoyed the pervading atmosphere and 'delicious' odour – all the time listening to the 'deadly music of the machine guns'. A nurse asks Etienne to assist in bringing people to the safety of the underground cellars. He does so every evening until, tragically, he is mortally wounded, riddled with shrapnel.

"Le Cocher de Reims" (The Cabbie of Reims) takes the narrator (and the reader) and on a seven-kilometre guided tour of the bombed city in his light horse-drawn carriage. It is the 372nd day of bombardment! His commentary covers details of casualties, destroyed buildings and various activities of the people, including the fact that the children are schooled in the cellars 'amid thousands of bottles of champagne'. Unlike many others, he had not left Reims wanting to stay close to his wife who was buried in the cemetery, so far undisturbed by the 'Boches'. 'If the trenches are full of heroes and the battlefields strewn with them, there are plenty in the occupied areas and the bombarded towns', according to the narrator. And the cabbie claims the people in Reims are 'citizen *poilus* who are at the Front, without being there'.

The remaining three stories in this collection are included here.

In *Choses d'hier*, Wenz concentrates on similar and other aspects of life in the Champagne district including the horrific destruction caused by the enemy's persistent bombardment, hospital material and food needs and the flow of hoards of people – citizens, soldiers and refugees – to and from the city. "La Dernière" and "A la campagne" – both autobiographical with a first person narrator – conclude with a solitary figure: an old woman who refuses to join the people leaving the city since she doesn't fear the Germans who had invaded in 1870 when she was young. She is captured, bound and questioned about the entrance to the underground tunnels. Proudly, she refuses to answer and is brutally executed receiving twelve bullets in her frail body 'when a slap in the face would have sufficed'.

In the other story, the narrator/ Paul, forced to work as a driver for the Germans when they occupied the area, had to carry evidence of his status: 'Monsieur has permission to drive in Reims and the surrounding districts requisitioning milk for the wounded and delivering to the hospitals'. The Germans were withdrawing from the area. They had occupied dwellings in the country town of Jonchery-sur-Vesle, sixteen kilometres from Reims, where the Wenz family owned cottages. On checking, Paul finds nothing damaged only signs they had been occupied; his brothers' cellars, however, had been emptied. Among the chaos, there were children's toys that were in pieces, dolls without their heads or limbs – 'more horrible to see than clothes strewn everywhere and trampled by large dirty boots'. In the stable, he finds a Boche dead drunk, asleep on the straw and snoring; he had taken off his gear, his uniform and his boots. He is locked in with a bottle of fine champagne and a loaf of bread waiting for the troops to leave and is then taken prisoner by the French authorities and made to unload coal at Dieppe, or flour in Rouen.

The other stories tell of a shepherd ("Le Berger") who doesn't like people, but spends an entire night watching over a field of fifty lifeless soldiers, 'their souls having left through their wounds'. They had given their all to defend the fields where his sheep pastured. In "R.F.C". (Royal Flying Corps), 'Herbert was everything a man ought to be who had the honour of being part of the R.F.C.'. In his free time, he loved walking in Hyde Park where convalescents came to enjoy the sun. Here, he meets a young woman and their friendship begins: she in admiration of the bravery of airmen and Herbert agreeing with her. After several outings and a proposal of marriage, word comes that he has had an accident. She visits the base to discover he is a mere cook and not the imagined brave airman he let her believe him to be. When he explains that he too risks being injured, she begins to cry – tears that meant that there was still hope for their relationship to continue.

"La Peur" is set in an uninhabited château where three Germans, a colonel and two soldiers, spend the night despite the rumour that it is haunted. But the colonel is frightened of nothing! He decides to sleep alone in the large dining room after wining and dining with other officers and sending the two soldiers to spend the night in the concierge's quarters. In a show of bravado, the colonel toasts to the ghosts. Later alone, he looks around him at the portraits of former brave Frenchmen, including a hussar in Napoleon's army, and finds an iron handcuff attached to the wall. Curious as to how it works, he places it on his wrist and closes the catch. Unfortunately, no matter how hard he tried, he cannot unlock it and, as the candles extinguish one by one, he is left in the dark: 'Suddenly, a window opens with a loud bang letting the room be filled with wind ...'. 'With the wind and the moonlight, Fear entered'!

A soldier ("Le Filleul") decides to write to two 'godmothers' (*marraines*) who complement each other: the soldier, nicknamed 'bigamist' among the other soldiers, receives letters and parcels from both. One sends practical items such as socks and a jumper; the other chooses extras like chocolate and tobacco. He imagines what they look like and how they live. To pass time in the trenches and back from the Front, he makes and sends two rings – each with a heart entwined with ivy leaves bearing his initials. In hospital blinded, he writes to his 'godmothers' who visit.

"D.S.O." (Distinguished Services Order), renamed "D.C.M." (Distinguished Conduct Medal),[23] is the story of an Englishman who returns from Canada and receives a commission in the army. He spends six months waiting to be sent to the Front. When he is notified that he is to replace an officer killed in battle, he is relieved that he will at last be contributing to the 'great task'. But he too is wounded in his first skirmish. He learns that, while Sergeant Samon was carrying him from the trench to safety, Samon had been wounded twice. The narrator explains Benjamin Samon's Jewish heritage, from his grandfather Isaac Solomon to his father Henry Salmon, giving details of their London businesses and their change of name. Benjamin Samon had a profitable men's clothing business. On leaving hospital, Benjamin Samon received a bravery award he believed he deserved no more than many others.

*

Walter Gow, Paul's estate manager on his property Nanima, received a letter dated 9 December 1918 from Paul: 'We have been living in a sort of dream since the fateful 11th November. For a week London went mad, and behaved like a larrikin; but nobody minded anything, and it was good to see'. According to him, Paris had a 'more dignified' Armistice Day. Later, he had joined the official group at Charing Cross to meet General Ferdinand Foch, the Supreme Commander of the Allied forces, and the French Prime Minister Georges Clemenceau on their arrival in London: 'The welcome of the two men was frantic'.[24]

Writing from Le Chesnay (Ile de France) on August 7, 1919, Paul Wenz described the Victory March of 14 July: 'Paris was full to bursting ... The allies had all their share of ovations': Yankees, Belgians, Italians, British, Scots and French. He was most impressed with decorations at the Rond Point of the Champs Elysees:

> At each side of this place there was a small mountain made of German guns, heaped and dropped anyhow – tails up, mouths up – just as the steam crane let them go. It was just two enormous heaps of scrap iron. On top of one was a huge cock on the defensive, 1914; on the top of the other, another cock crowing 1919.

When it was over, 'Paris was hoarse, tired and stiff-necked. But Paris was satisfied ... The 'poilus' had had their day; some of them reckoned it was worth years of fighting to get under the Arc de Triomphe'.[25]

'So the years passed. Though Europe heaved and changed politically, at Nanima the seasons were the same. For Paul and Hettie, life was vital, precious, not to be wasted'.[26] Paul continued writing. He published a document in 1925 on raising sheep in Australia, *Elevage du mouton en Australie. Décrit en vue de son application dans les colonies françaises* (Librairie Emile Larose) illustrated by his brother Frédéric; a novel in 1929 set in the Great Barrier Reef of Queensland, *Le Jardin des coraux* (Calmann-Lévy); an autobiography the following year, *Il était une fois un gosse* and in 1931 *L'Echarde* (Editions de la Vraie France), the latter translated by Maurice Blackman as *The Thorn in the Flesh* (Imprint 2004).

Not long after Paul Wenz died, France was again invaded by German troops.

NOTES

[1] Denis Wenz, *Emile Wenz "Lainier" 1834-1926* (1998), RCP Coulon, Cergy, 2015, 25-26.

[2] Paul Wenz, *Il était une fois un gosse*, Editions de la Vraie France, Paris, 1930, 64; 'A mes frères: EMILE, FREDERIC, ALFRED, JOSEPH, A ma sœur ALINE Affectueusement P. W.'

[3] D Wenz, *Emile Wenz*, 15; P Wenz, *Il était une fois*, 66-74; 143-4.

[4] Marion Ord, 'Paul Wenz, The Master of Nanima', Radio play produced by Peter Whitlock for *The Land and its People* on 2CY & 2NC, 8.30pm, 13 October 1961, *Canberra Times*, <http://trove.nla.gov.au>, 4-5. For information about the Wenz collection of books, see: <merril.findlay.com>.

[5] Maurice Blackman, 'Paul Wenz (1869-1939). French-Australian Writer and Grazier', in Eric Berti & Ivan Barko, *French Lives in Australia*, Australian Scholarly, North Melbourne, 2015, 280.

[6] Ord, 'Paul Wenz…', 7.

[7] See Richard Waterhouse, 'The Pioneer Legend and its Legacy: In Memory of John Hirst', *Journal of the Royal Australian Historical Society*, vol.103, pt 1, 2017, 7-25.

[8] Paul Warrego, *A l'autre bout du monde. Aventures et mœurs Australiennes* (capital A for the adjective – Australian – shows confusion between French and English rules), Librairie Universelle, Paris, 1905. 'En Nouvelle Calédonie', 'Une soirée à Tonga', 'Fausse alerte', 'Le Trader' and 'Faruma' are not set in Australia.

[9] Paul Wenz, *Sous la Croix du Sud. Contes Australiens*, Plon, Paris, 1911; 'Tallicolo', set in 1878 on an island in the Pacific, and 'Samoa' which continues the narrative of 'Faruma'.

[10] Paul Warrego, *Diary of a New Chum*, McCarron, Bird & Co, Melbourne, 1908. Preface by Frank Moorhouse in Paul Wenz, *Diary of a New Chum and Other Lost Stories*, edited by Maurice Blackman, Angus & Robertson, Nth Ryde, 1990. 2.

[11] For example: Arthur Upfield, author of the Detective Napoleon Bonaparte (Boney) stories, arrived as a "new chum" from England, enlisted in the military and returned to live permanently

in Australia; the 1944 film by Charles Chauvel *The Rats of Tobruk* has Australian actor Peter Finch playing the English "new chum" experiencing bush life as a drover and then enlisting with his mates in the army in WWII.

[12] 'L'homme ne peut créer sans torturer ni sans détruire', "Le Vagabond", Wenz, *A l'autre bout*, 11;

[13] Letter to André Gide, nov. 9, 1916, 9 Kingsbridge, Hyde Park Corner, in Paul Wenz, *Le Pays de leurs pères*, La Petite Maison, Paris, 1996, 198; dedication: 'To the men who came from Australia and New Zealand to fight with us. In memory of those who our French soil will watch over'. At least 45,000 of the 295,000 Australians who fought in France died; casualties were estimated at 226,000. The first edition was titled *Au pays de leurs pères*.

[14] Ord, 'Paul Wenz', 7.

[15] Wenz, *Il était une fois*, 55-6.

[16] Paul Wenz, 'Rheims During the Bombardment', *Lone Hand*, March 1915, 250-1; also in 'At the War', *Forbes Times*, 23 March 1915.

[17] Letter to André Gide, mars 9, 1916, 196-7.

[18] 'Lost Hospitals of London', <http://ezitis.myzen.co.uk/secondlondon.html>.

[19] St Dunstan's Hospital London, <archives@blindveterans.org.uk>.

[20] Letter to Gide, 30 juillet 1917, 199-200. The address given was Londres, 9 Knightsbridge S W; earlier as 9 Knightsbridge, Hyde Park Corner. In this letter, Wenz points out that the war had broken down social-class barriers especially among Australians.

[21] 'Mr. Paul Wenz', *Sydney Stock and Station Journal*, 3 January 1919.

[22] *Illustration*, no 3978, 31 mai 1919, in Paul Wenz, *Le Trader*, La Petite Maison, Paris, 2006, 28-9.

[23] In my copy of *Choses d'hier*, a member of the Wenz family had written: 'Nouvelle à supprimer'. Beneath the Table of Contents of the book was written: 'If Paul had experienced the Shoah, he would have been ASHAMED to have written [this story].'

[24] '"Der Tag" Foch and Clemenceau in London. Interesting Letter from Mr Paul Wenz', *Forbes Advocate*, 4 March 1919.

[25] 'March of Victory Great Paris Procession. Mr Paul Wenz's Description', *Forbes Advocate*, 17 October 1919.

[26] Narrator, Ord, 'Paul Wenz', 8.

THEIR FATHERS' LAND

(Le pays de leurs pères)

A NOVEL

CHAPTER I

Spanish, Dutch, English and French navigators took it upon themselves to name a large portion of the Australian coastline. Explorers who penetrated the mysterious and inhospitable interior of the continent named the rivers, creeks, plains and the mountains they crossed. Next came the pioneers, squatters and miners who chose Aboriginal names, or ones that reminded them of the "old country", to places they designated. Sometimes it was the name of a small hamlet in England, or a tiny town where they were born. For them, it was an echo of the past for they felt the emigrant's nostalgia having left Europe behind with no hope of ever seeing it again. Some places were given the name of an object found in the area. The discovery of an old pot of zinc had its importance in these isolated places. It indicated that a white man had passed that way. And so there are several *Tin Pot Creek*s in Australia and *Tin Pot Station*s, here and there.

The capital cities were named after important men, soldiers or explorers. Fortunately, Aboriginal names are still numerous; they are generally pleasant-sounding, sonorous and gracious while maintaining a tribal note. A Sydney cove, Woolloomooloo – perhaps suggesting cannibals – has a record number of eight "o"s.

The boss at *Lone Man Plain* has in his office an old notebook with yellow tattered pages that explain the origins of the station and the reason it got its name.

17 October 1867. Camp No XV: Today we did about nineteen miles. Harry's packhorse is injured in the withers; we had to lighten its load by giving some to my horse Billy. We camped beside a creek with clear water without mosquitoes. Harry shot a bush turkey and two bronze pigeons that are going to give us a different meal from the usual. We think we'll reach the river sometime tomorrow. We'll cross it and hopefully find the beautiful plain which we vaguely heard about in Melbourne. Yesterday for the first time, we noticed signs of the Blacks. Today there are even more. We saw trees where they have cut into the bark so they can climb up looking for possums or wild honey. There are ritual patterns cut deep into the trunks. It's hard to know what these represent, but make us think of a labyrinth. They are probably their own particular form of writing.

18 October. Camp No XVI: This morning, an hour after leaving camp, we discovered marks in some trees made by a steel axe. The cut into the bark was already several months old; it was clean and the bark had not yet formed a hard edge. We followed these blazes that are seen quite clearly and indicate a precise set direction. As we left the camp where we had lunch, the marks still showed the way to the river. Harry and I weren't very pleased to see these indications of the presence of a white man in the area. The man had preceded us and had perhaps taken possession of our promised land!

The forest we are going through is not what we call a forest in Europe. The eucalyptus trees are set wide apart as their roots need room to run along the surface and then plunge down deeply to find their subsistence. At first sight, this gives the impression of a huge park or of a gigantic orchard. It is easy to ride on horseback between the trunks and the greyish-green foliage gives shade which is a little like a thin gauze between us and the sun.

After lunch, we finally reached the river. It is wide with steep banks. On the sides that slope gently, the trees are gathered like a flock of animals hurrying to drink. Their roots, which the river high tides have exposed, twist on the surface like monstrous serpents. They look as though they are interlocked in battle, escaping and then crawling to disappear beneath the water. The river is obstructed by dead giants and their big black arms that come out of the current seem to belong to drowned men.

In this isolated country silence is suddenly torn apart by the cry of a cockatoo that saw us and quickly gave the alarm. Others answered leaving the top of a tall tree in a cloud of large white petals flying over our heads. A crane is perched on a dead branch while a water bird, which looked like a snake swimming, disappeared into the water and surfaced twenty-five yards further along.

Our horses are drinking. Our dog is in the water and is drinking as if he wants to swallow the entire river. He expresses his contentment by joyfully barking and once again upsetting the deep silence. Will throws a branch at his head to silence him for we both feel we want to look at this river in its entire mysterious natural setting as yet untouched, as yet not really awakened.

We were strolling along the bank when Harry first notices a grey tent in the distance. As we get closer we see the tent is torn. Closer still we notice a pile of ashes, cut wood and a small table made from a piece of bark held up on four y-shaped sticks. Plates and small tin cans are placed there but are covered in rust and leaves. Inside the tent, under some dusty blankets is a dried-out form that was once a man. It was merely a mummified thing, dry like dead wood. The corpse was not terrible to look at for the man's profile was intact, emaciated like a mask that had taken its rest after experiencing all the suffering the earth can offer men.

Behind the tent, a rusty chain attached to a pole held the mummified form of a dog still with its collar on. Its teeth shone in the sun.

19 October. Camp No XVII: I swim across the river to see if it is free from tree trunks and stumps that shag; then we take the two saddle horses and the two other horses without their packs across. After tying up the horses, we go back for our bags and precious rations which we take to the other side in small quantities, making several trips. We are mediocre as tightrope walkers and cannot risk carrying the sugar and flour on our heads, so we have to carry our bundles in one hand and use the other to swim. The current is rather strong and this takes us the whole morning. We inspect the plain north of the river. It is just what we were hoping to find. We saw it stretching as far as the horizon, with curtains of tall trees cut in the east and the west, perhaps indicative of creek beds. We see salt bush, cotton bush and mulga, and others – we don't know their names. There are hills of pink sand where bunches of pines are growing. It all has the appearance of good terrain for cattle and sheep.

21, 22, 23, 24, 25 October: We leave the river and, compass in hand, head directly north for a distance of some thirty miles... With an axe we cut a right angle in the earth and place a large stake marked with our initials H[arry] L[ewis] M[ills]. As a precaution against fire, we destroy the grass for several yards around the post.

Then we go east for twenty miles or so and mark another right angle, insert another post and set the compass to the south back to the river.

In this way we have a large rectangle which we cut diagonally twice to give us an idea of the area. We were not mistaken. The plain is everything we could have wished for. There is wood in abundance with low hills and above flood level. Grass is plentiful and varied. We didn't notice any area burnt by salt or alkali, or low-lying sections denuded by the persistent presence of water.

We went past a camp of Blacks who fled as we came near. Only one old man with a long white beard came towards us with his arms held up probably to show us he didn't have any weapons. Twenty yards from me, he lifted his right heel suddenly and seized a spear he was holding between his toes. Fortunately Harry was on the alert and the shot he fired in the air frightened the old man and his spear missed me by six feet. He left us as masters of the terrain and disappeared behind the trees along the creek. These blacks will probably give us sufficient reasons to react. We intend to kill Aborigines only as a last resort. There are too many Whites who shoot them as if they were game.

The journal ends here abruptly.

Six months later, Harry and Lewis Mills took possession of nearly half a million acres (approx. 200 000 hectares) of land, taking their families and the men who were to work for them and leading 1,200 heads of cattle. Years were needed to transform this immense plain into pastoral land.

Horses soon appeared on the scene, then wire fences were erected and sheep came bleating among the salt bush and settled not far from the shaded creeks.

From time to time, the Blacks killed an ox or a calf and the tribe had a regal meal that lasted several days. But the Mills were honest and humane conquerors. They thought the best hunting grounds of the Aborigines had been taken by white men. They killed kangaroos with their guns, chased game at a distance making it difficult for the man who had only a spear and a boomerang. The Mills were among the first men to frequently distribute, on a regular basis, rations of sugar, flour tobacco and blankets to the Aborigines on the station. Some accepted work paid for in kind. The shop even became at certain times a meeting place, especially when the head of the tribe suddenly decided that the black skin of his wives, although decorated with tattoos *en relief,* was no longer to be considered as suitable clothing.

When in 1880 the young generation of Mills took over the management of the station from their elders, *Lone Man Plain* had 80,000 sheep, 5,000 heads of cattle and 1,200 horses. The brand *"Lone Man Plain across a boomerang"* was well known among wool buyers and was still highly thought of at the London sales.

The paddocks had multiplied; water conservation had been studied with the result that each of the forty-five paddocks had a creek, the river or a damn to water the herds. The first homestead had been built on the river. The men's huts, the stables, barns and sheds, the blacksmith's and the carpenter's workshops made up an agglomeration of whitened roofs that, in the middle of the greenery of the tall trees and orange trees in the garden, was a true village. A huge shed, where fifty shearers did the mechanised shearing, had been recently constructed along the river bank. And the wool pressed into bails held together with iron straps was loaded onto large barges which a steamboat tugged eight hundred miles to the open sea.

In spring, *Lone Man Plain* could be a huge park with the grass full of buttercups, Easter daisies and blue bellflowers. The wattles in bloom seemed like magical trees where ingots of the most beautiful gold had sprouted. Lambs frisking about everywhere put the finishing touch to the scene.

Then the warm summer winds arrived. In one week the grass became reddish-brown and the water in the creeks began to diminish. Swarms of flies were in the air annoying men and beasts from dawn to dusk. Summer quickly took its place and the sun became a monstrous divinity everyone wanted to avoid and escape from. Blazing hot winds swept over the country and, for months, people were frightened of fire when there was plenty of dry grass and of famine when there was hardly any. They would constantly look at the sky. It was the most beautiful pale blue, but promised nothing.

At last, summer ended. All nature and her creatures blessed the first showers. Winter brought in cold nights and something like a European spring sun. Sometimes, there were floods that drowned animals and destroyed fences.

The man who lived in this perpetual struggle with the atmospheric forces ended up playing his part despite himself for he was always forced to take risks. The player became a philosopher as he lost quite often even if he began with the best trumps. After each loss, he reshuffled the cards and started hoping once again for good fortune.

Persistent bad luck rarely makes him give up. Each year seems to bring a new scourge, another enemy to do battle with. The Australian climate seems to be marvellously adapted to experiments on the increase in numbers of rabbits, foxes and sparrows which are as much the plagues of Egypt introduced by good people who had the best intentions in the world. It is said that one day a good woman brought to Australia a small pot containing a cactus from a far-off country. It was a novelty. She gave cuttings to many of her friends and this new indoor plant became very fashionable. Unfortunately for Australia, the plant left the homes and invaded certain regions of Queensland and New South Wales, so much so that the government will lease, for almost nothing, land that is invaded by the prickly-pear cactus, on the proviso that you destroy this very hardy ornamental plant.

At first, the workers at *Lone Man Plain* formed a strange group. There were a few former convicts who were at the time leading a very peaceful and patriarchal life looking after sheep that had been entrusted to them. Old Jackson walked with a heavy cadenced tread. Some claimed that this came from his long stay at Parramatta in the work gang where his feet were in chains. Nevertheless, Jackson seemed the most honest of men and, if he had been sent to Australia at the age of seventeen by King George IV for stealing a goose, it seemed to indicate above everything that the deceased king was particularly interested in fowl.

A former whaler who had roamed the seas of the globe had arrived at the station where he had no difficulty in finding work for he could do carpentry, woodworking, forging, even cooking. He was a jack-of-all-trades – a conscientious, honest worker. His only vice was tobacco which he chewed and smoked equally, but couldn't do without for a minute.

There was also a university-educated man who, for reasons that concerned no one, had given up his books to look after merinos. It wasn't known if sometimes he recited Virgil during the long lonely daylight hours, but it was known that, when a bottle of rum mysteriously came his way in his small hut, university English changed to a language that smacked more of tar than of wild flowers.

CHAPTER II

Living in the Australian bush is to live as close to nature as possible, since man is constantly in touch with it. Often alone, far away from others, he has to battle using his own strength. Birth, life and death are reduced to their simplest forms. The bushman is a type of primitive: he comes into the world, lives with what is given him and leaves quietly, as if unwilling to upset anyone.

The immense desert plains, the dried-up creeks left behind by gold prospectors, the telegraph line that crosses Australia for more than two thousand kilometres from the south to the north, have seen him seeking his fortune in lonely places where water is scarce and nothing can save him from hunger. He thinks simply that the moment has come for him. He closes his eyes to get used to the great obscurity into which he will be dragged.

Jim Clarke came on this earth, unannounced, and his mother bravely bore the anxieties and agonies that are the exorbitant cost Nature demands for a poor, little human being to enter this world. The bark hut was in the full sun. In the shade, a reliable thermometer would have indicated 115° Fahrenheit that day.

For the previous two weeks, Bill, the husband, a boundary rider of *Lone Man Plain*, had been away with other stockmen rounding up cattle. He had written to alert Mrs Brown, the women's helper, of the situation. She covered the entire district the size of four French *départements*. At the last moment, the helper was of course not able to be there. Tiny Jim announced his arrival without too much fuss, but loud enough for his mother to know he was equipped to face life. When the new-born was exactly 48 hours old, the helper arrived on a lame horse which had had its eyes attacked by flies. Although late, she was none-theless welcome.

The child was eleven days old when he was presented to his father. Two years later, Jim was baptised. A parson arrived and stopped his horse-drawn carriage in front of the hut. Having set out at sunrise, he was covered in dust after his forty-five-mile journey across the plain. Bill did what he could to give the parson the least possible rustic hos-pitality. But the hut was small, water was scarce and every drop had to be carried from the creek. The parson had a tent set up under a large tree. A few blows with an axe and the boundary rider had made a simple bed for him.

It was an unadorned baptismal ceremony. With disconcerting indif-ference, the infant was given the names James Arthur as his forehead was anointed with water from Cockatoo Creek – the trees along its banks could be seen some two hundred yards away.

Mrs Bill Clarke prepared a dinner of salted beef and tinned potatoes as the main course. The fact that *Lone Man Plain* had five thousand cattle did not prevent Swiss cows providing thick condensed milk in small round tins. The milk was dissolved in a very strong and very sugary tea. The parson was given the cup of honour, the only cup in the place. Bill and his wife each had a tin pannikin, well-seasoned like a smoker's pipe, by very strong tea made from water tasting of gum leaves which fell into the creek bed. A robust jam pudding for dessert didn't prevent the parson finishing the meal. Then, on a beautiful, calm night with the creek frogs croaking incessantly, the two men smoked their pipes and chatted about the season, the surrounding farms and Australian politics – one of the world's phenomena.

The parson spoke about his rounds in a district that took him six months to cover – carrying out a church service here and there in a tiny corrugated-iron roofed chapel. But generally his congregations were in station homesteads, or the working men's hut.

He met poverty along the way, but it was never extreme. The people were always able to satisfy their hunger. There was an amazing patient philosophy everywhere in the bush: bad seasons ruined some graziers, but they always hoped to hear rain falling and then they would begin again, never totally discouraged. The parson was a humane, kindly man whose dark frockcoat was worn and stained in places and the long journey in his buggy had removed any sign of stiffness or severity.

The clergyman (*Reverend*) had a beard and the bright eyes of a man living in the sun-flooded plains that enlivened his wise and friendly *bon enfant* face. "No, my friends", he said as he left them to sleep in his tent. "I don't want anything. You have been cordial and openly welcoming and I have gained another parishioner. I take money only from the rich for charity. You don't owe me anything. Thank you again for your hospitality. Good night."

The next day, Bill had the horses harnessed and, after a solid breakfast, the parson was on his vagabond way after waving goodbye with his whip to his one-night hosts.

Jim was three, and almost too big for the recycled raison container that, until then, was used as his cradle, when a remarkable thing happened in the district – rain fell. For an entire day, the sky cried as if it was repenting for having allowed so many cattle and sheep to die and Bill took great pleasure in deliberately getting soaking wet, so much so that his raincoat, which had been hanging on a nail for months, absolutely refused to bend. It split from top to bottom like a piece of dried bark.

Young Jim went out on the veranda and was really surprised to see what was falling from the roof while the water container, which had been empty for such a long time, was filling up with a rather frightening cavernous thudding sound. The child looked at the damp veranda floor as if it were the bridge of a boat being hosed down. Visibly worried, he called his mother and asked her how she was going to clean the floor. She smiled and explained that the rain was water falling from the sky.

Jim then learnt about mud for he rolled off the veranda onto the naked pink earth where the persistent raindrops were exploding! Stained from head to feet, he went back into the hut in triumph to be welcomed by a laughing mother for she considered mud a beautiful thing, a good thing and the cleanest thing in the world when it is earth joined with water!

For rain is manna – a blessing from heaven; it is the fairy that makes grass grow in three days, that fills the water barrels, creeks and rivers, that gives the atmosphere an odour that only the sky can give. Tiny Jim learnt about rain that day. He learnt to love and wish for it like the genuine good Australian he was.

The hut began to crumble to pieces; a varied entomological collection – from giant spiders to equally giant millipedes – was found under the pieces of bark used for the roof. While a gap resembling a mouse hole, but was actually used by a brown snake, gave the floor a haunted appearance that had disturbed Jim's mother's sleep more than once. The snake had had its spiny backbone broken in two places by a whip and the hole had been blocked. But the whip still hung on its nail in case it was needed.

Bill started to build a small cottage with material the homestead station sent him. Like sailors and bushmen, he did a little renovating. He had done some iron-mongering, planing and trowel work. He took pleasure in building a new dwelling. The spot he chose was barely a few yards from the old hut and he began setting foundation blocks made from biscuit boxes that were often used in the Australian bush. A light frame of laths was prepared to support a galvanised iron roof which was screwed or hammered on, depending on whether a person was working for himself or for a boss. A saw, a hammer, wire-cutters and a screwdriver were all that were needed to build such a house in the country.

It was not long before Bill had finished mortising the wood and assembling it to make a long, light but solid frame. The hammer began its noise, hitting the awl and making holes for the screws. This work did not stop from dawn to dusk on one particular Sunday. The walls and the roof were in place; the building looked like a brand new doll's house by its architectural simplicity and smelling of native pines. The doors and windows took time to be added as they came from far away. A wrap-around veranda on the sides provided precious shade. Then Bill put in the lining of tongue-and-groove planks and the floor. He built the hearth from solid earth covered with stones and the brick chimney.

Moving house took a morning. The furniture – it must be said – was not complicated. Bill hung up a lamp, added a plank above the hearth on which he placed a few photos he had framed himself, two emu eggs he had engraved, using a few pieces of silex found during his rides, and a dried iguana with its mouth open. It had been suffocated by a crow when it greedily tried to swallow it.

The few colour prints that had been in the hut were carefully unscrewed, cleaned and reappeared in places of honour on the new wooden wall. They were part of the family fortune. Their intrinsic value was that of illustrated newspaper supplements several years old, but an entire past was linked to these engravings held in the garish colours that smoke over four years had patinated – similar to old Rembrandts.

Bill had to demolish the original flimsy bark hut built especially for his wife. He could have put a match to it, but that seemed brutal and there may have been a superstitious reason. The large strips of bark were taken off one by one. He took down the shutters with their hinges made from beef hide; he took off the old door undoing the simple latch he had made from a piece of iron-hard red gum.

The old floor he carefully removed, not forgetting the brown snake which was pleasantly surprised. He found the first brooch he had given to his wife that she had lost three years earlier. The old hut seemed to appreciate the man who had spared it until the very last moment.

One Saturday when Bill was going to the homestead for provisions, Mrs Mills wanted to know what stage the new house had reached. Bill took this advantage to ask the boss's wife for any old illustrated newspapers to line the walls with. Mrs Mills gave him huge bundles of *Graphics* and *Illustrated News* which he was really pleased to accept.

A book should be written entitled "About the influence of the environment in general and wallpaper in particular on the morale and character of people". A shorter title could of course appear at the beginning of the volume.

How many children can remember the impossible daubing of paper that was used to cover, without decorating, the walls of their small bedrooms? Flowers resembling grotesque fish, impossible insects or grimacing, nightmarish faces. How many remember pretentious and ridiculous minuets with people in wigs and carrying baskets, who greeted each other 167 times in the room with the same gestures like poorly-jointed puppets – 167 times not counting the twenty-six groups that the frieze on top had cut off and the plinth had rendered legless?

Bill's efforts and the flour paste his wife made in large quantities were not lost. The room, used as a dining, living and smoking room, was brightened up by multiple scenes from the four corners of the earth, all different, and where some interesting new detail was discovered every day.

These walls were Jim's first school lessons. He gleaned from them a harvest of questions, often embarrassing the parents when the detail did not appear under the engraving. He quickly learned to recognise Queen Victoria, in Hyde Park, in a carriage, in the mountains of Scotland or on a yacht anchored in the waters of the Isle of Wight.

The bedroom was an encyclopaedia: history, geography, science, art, zoology, astronomy – all were there. Turkish sponge fishermen were found next to wolf hunting in Prussia, a drawing-room in Buckingham Palace was beside an underground scene of diamond mines in South Africa. An eruption in Krakatoa touched a polar landscape marvellously decorated with white bears and seals. It was a series of brisk jumps, of magical journeys from one end of the world to the other. After a few days, Bill revealed an ambition, the first he had ever seriously had. He wanted to be rich to see the world, to travel a little everywhere. His wife would have liked to see the Queen and the royal family in their finest attire, crowned and covered in diamonds and pearls. She wanted to attend a service in Westminster Abbey. The call of "home", of the motherland, had reached them as second generation Australians. They dreamt of the "old country" their ancestors had left. These old newspapers were a sudden revelation!

The Australian has a blind love for his country and, in general, a desire to see the old world if ever, whenever the opportunity arises. Young Jim learned the word Europe early. Bill had suddenly discovered he knew nothing of English History. He wrote to the city and had books sent to him. The shelf he had nailed as a library soon became insufficient for he wanted to learn the history and geography of other countries.

When the boy could stand firmly on his legs, it was thought it would soon be time to put him on a saddle. At five years of age, he had his own pony and would bring in the dairy cow grazing in the small paddock next to the house for his mother. The dogs were his first friends. Then there was a joey, a young kangaroo Bill had brought home from one of his rounds. Its mother had miscalculated her jump and had caught her two back paws in the fence and had died entangled in the twisted wires. The young roo, patiently fed, learnt very quickly and had instinctively assumed the attitude of a boxer towards the dogs and they respected it.

A cockatoo was also part of the family. The disconcerting habit of being everywhere had resulted in a small chain being placed on its leg, for it was like its peers – the feathered demons of destruction. Every now and then, Bill would dismount in front of the house veranda and the child knew by the look on his father's face that there was an imminent surprise for him. Once the boundary rider took from under his shirt a sweet little black rabbit that he handed to Jim for one day only as Australian law punished anyone breeding or keeping rabbits in captivity demanding a hefty fine. The bunny drank milk from a teaspoon at first and the next day the child kissed its snout and said goodbye and "bunny", without knowing it, went on to the eternity full of small Australian rabbits.

CHAPTER III

He was only seven when his father took him to the homestead complex for the first time. The ride was long for a child, more than twenty-five miles, but Jim thought it an exciting privilege and didn't notice the distance. If he did feel a little tired, he quickly forgot when they reached the station. He had never seen such an array of buildings. He had never seen so many people gathered at the one time.

As he followed his father into the boss's house, it seemed that his father was dwarfed by the high ceilings, the grandeur and number of the rooms. He noticed the etchings on the walls. There were not as many as at his place, nor were they as interesting. There was a dog looking at a horse whose head was visible above a stable door; there was another with a man and a woman both strangely dressed and talking to each other. She was mending something while he was using a stick to draw in the sand in the laneway. There were also portraits of people who were not at all pleasant looking. Jim noticed a number of chairs, armchairs, tables, a huge mirror, where you could see yourself from head to toe, and shelves full of books.

The boss and his wife came into the smoking room. Jim held out his hand without looking at anyone and without opening his mouth. Then he sat on a chair and looked at the mat with flowers as if he had never seen any before. The tea brought in gave rise to a new and interesting topic. There was a silver teapot, a cup with a blue pattern and shiny spoons. But he admired the cake most. A large piece was cut for him which he ate, letting the crumbs fall onto the beautiful flowers. After two cups of well-sugared tea, he felt very good and familiarised himself to his surroundings.

A little while later, they stood up and he was taken across the garden where the woman gathered two oranges for him. He put them in separate pockets. Jim would have liked a third one to eat straightaway, but he resolutely hid these feelings. The garden was interesting. There were hedges of rose bushes covered with blooms; other flowers of every colour with bees buzzing above them. He said goodbye and went with his father to the men's shed, then to the store where he saw bags of flour and sugar, jars of all kinds of conserves lined the shelves, while from the ceiling hung billies, pannikins and axe handles. The storekeeper gave him a highly-colourful picture that came from a box of American tobacco.

Suddenly a raucous whistle rang out. The storekeeper said: "That's the *Mooljoola*". They went out and, fifty yards from there, they came to the riverbank. Jim had seen only the back paddock creeks with water that was like a dark mirror under the tall trees. But this water was flowing; it was yellow like strong, milky tea; it was wide and disappeared a few hundred yards around a sharp elbow.

His father pointed out something coming up the river. At first, he saw a lot of smoke coming from what seemed to be a white house, flat like a box. The house came closer and grew bigger. Jim could hear a regular repeated sound; the water was being disturbed on both sides of the house. At last, he could see the paddle – shut in a cage as dangerous beasts are – beating the river, the high black chimney belching out sparks. On the roof of the white house there were some men who were making signs and calling out. A white spray came from the front of the chimney and another raucous whistle floated over the water overhung by the tall trees and chased a cloud of grey and pink galahs into the pale blue sky. Ropes were thrown; the house stopped and was tied to two large gum trees.[1]

A plank was placed on the bank and straightaway flour bags, jute sacks for wool and rolls of wire were unloaded. Jim didn't know where to look. The thunderous wheel caught his attention. He went closer to the large cage where the beast that had hit the water was now sleeping. He could see several large fins still dripping with water. A boat. It was a paddle steamer that had come from the open salty sea. It had travelled up the mighty Murray and the Darling Rivers for about eight hundred miles taking weeks to make the journey.

After dinner, Jim found his bed in the men's hut next to his father. It wasn't long before he was asleep despite the continuing conversations and the pipe smoke filling the large room with its blue fog.

The next morning, he had to get on his horse to go back home. He found time to go to the river, but the *Mooljoola* had already left in the night following the meandering of the river towards Bourke. The 'white house' had disappeared like a dream, but Jim knew it wasn't a dream and he promised himself he would see the boat again.

The child thought the return ride was short; the horses knew too that they were returning to their paddock, their creek, their home. Bill had to answer many questions on navigation, the power of the motor and the internal workings of boats in general. To Jim's amazement, who did not really understand how men could sleep in a bed on a boat while it was moving, Bill recounted how his grandfather had come from the "old country" in 1868 on a sailing boat that took five months. It had touched down at St Helena where the passengers had disembarked to visit the tomb of Napoleon Bonaparte. Many a weeping willow in Australia and New Zealand has grown from cuttings taken from the Longwood tree.[2]

---

[1] Mistranslation of gum trees as "gommiers", by Wenz.

[2] Longworth House was Napoleon's residence while on the island.

At one time the station of *Lone Man Plain* had accommodated fifteen children. The boss had a school built and a teacher came from Sydney to take charge of this horde. It was built in the most central position possible as the children were spread out in every direction. The lessons took place three times a week as a part-time or half-and-half school with another. Jim had twelve miles to travel on his pony. He left in the morning, with a bag crammed tight with his lunch and his school books, and headed towards Pelican Creek. The other children arrived also on horseback; one grey mare brought the three Perry children with the eldest being eleven years old. And when the mare had a pretty chestnut foal, the foal joined in and came to the school three times each week. The saddles were attached under a shed that kept them in the shade at least, even if it didn't stop the flies.

The schoolmaster was a very gentle man who seemed happy to have found a peaceful, simple task in this isolated spot. He quickly knew how to interest the children for he interested them from the very start even inculcating arithmetic by seasoning it with all types of spices to make it more attractive.

One day he set the following question:

Your garden is 15 yards long, a snake comes into the garden; it crawls one foot a second. How long will it take to get to your house?

"Never", young Mackenzie answered, "if our dog saw it".

He taught physics and chemistry by the simplest experiments. He did an autopsy on an old alarm clock and began an insect collection that before too long became the pride of the school.

Bob, the small Aboriginal boy of the camp, also wanted to go to school. He was the same age as Jim and had a very lively intelligence. His big dark eyes seemed to take in everything they saw. He had an amazing memory and had the advantage over his friends of being able to pick up his pen-holder without bending over for his toes had never been trapped in shoes. Bob was soon top of the children the same age.

His speech was still a little gobbledygook, devoid of articles, but always very expressive.

Bob also had an imagination that threatened to take him far. He lied, not maliciously, just for sport. But he lied a lot. One day the schoolmaster discovered Bob had a conscience that was, at times, quite obvious. When a dispute broke out or when the small boy was mixed up in an affair that needed some clarification, he was called to the teacher's desk at a set distance that enabled the teacher to see his pupil from his head to his toes.

"Bob, did you break Ted Nichols' slate?"

"No," the small Aborigine shook his ruffled head.

But the teacher wasn't looking at Bob's face; he was studying his feet, for with each lie his big toes moved as if they were in very hot water. Bob was sent back to his seat and deprived of recess. After a few episodes of this type of inquisition, Bob thought seriously about taking a further step into this marvellous civilisation that is ours and not go barefooted. But after wearing Tim Baxter's shoes for half a day, he concluded that sometimes freedom was well worth the price.

School years were short, for boys and girls had their chores at home. There were the cows to be brought in and milked, provisions to be got on horseback or by carriage. The mothers, who had to do endless washing, the cooking and making bread, were happy to have a helping hand especially when there were small ones to look after.

Moreover, the boys were in a hurry to begin their tasks as men: they cut wood with an American axe at an age that in Europe children were barely allowed to have even a blunt pocket knife. They already needed to earn a little money; they caught possums, rabbits and sold their skins; a little later, they helped in the yards to push sheep from one enclosure into another. They enrolled as rouseabouts when the shearing season began and took the wool that had been shorn to the table to be classified. Working among the men, they became manly almost as soon as they left school.

At first Jim followed behind his father on horseback along the wire fences he was responsible for maintaining in good condition. The kid began by learning how to repair the wire with a telegraphic knot, or a double flowing knot; he learnt how to tighten a wire that had become slack with the help of a horse or an ox. He knew how to replace broken poles like fixing broken legs, by binding them tightly between two strong splints.

The gates needed replacing. A wagon full of goods had knocked one of the posts and the unbalanced gate no longer shut firmly. One open fence gate on a station is something that is considered a calamity. It often means days of work, searching and rounding up. An Australian farmer always looks for ingenious locks that can be opened only by man. But some horses acquire man's imperfections except speaking and, after showing what patience they are capable of, are able to open the small latches that are considered inviolable.

It is then that the horse, so loved in Australia, forfeits its rights and is relegated to the ruminant family as a "cow". The same expression is used to describe a negligent or poorly intentioned wanderer who allows two herds to mix by not closing the paddock gate.

The job of the boundary rider who rides the length of the station boundaries is generally a solitary monotonous task. From morning to nightfall, he rides the fences looking all the time at the wires and the poles. When he covers twenty miles of fences in a day, he sees more than twelve thousand poles and something like ninety-three kilometres of wire.

The long horse ride in the full sun, when the only sound heard is the saddle creaking, allows the mind to wander. One thought follows another like the heavy shower of rain falling from dark clouds; memory, like a swollen bag, is full of everything stored away since it began in the mind. When the day is at its hottest, when the whole plain dances as if it was the bottom of a dazzling sea, when each small sandhill becomes a mountain and a stray goat seems the size of an ox, an evil *fairy* unfolds before your eyes a countryside of shade and running water.

Depending on the season, the boundary rider must also check if the sheep in a particular paddock have enough to drink; if the water in the hollowed-out earth dams is not too low and if the animals are not trapped in them. Sometimes his horse will swerve away as it goes by a sheep in agony. Bill gets down from the saddle and, if he realises that the animal cannot be saved, he cuts its throat and, wiping his knife blade on its wool, he watches its last spasms, the last signs of life flowing onto the dry earth. He lifts an eyelid with his thumb and the blank eye is the sign that it has ended. Then he cuts up the animal with the dexterity of a master butcher and attaches the skin to the back of his saddle leaving the skinned beast for the falcons and crows to feed on.

Then there are the lambs to be branded. A few months later, during the shearing, all the men are present when the sheep are gathered together. In each paddock, the men and their dogs form a chain that moves in a concentric pattern like the hand movement of a large clock pushing the sheep outside the paddock.

Gradually, Jim joins in with the men working in the dust of the yards in the suffocating shadow of the shearing shed when at any moment a response has to be given to the "sheep ho" of the shearers asking for another sheep. He even tried the mechanical shears on one animal. It vibrated in his closed hand like a snake fighting. His first impulse was to throw the thing which was warmed up by 380 revolutions a minute, snorting and vibrating like a mad animal. Under the shearer's directions, he had shredded a fleece while the animal fought since it was poorly held between his legs. His experience stopped there. He knew that O'Connor shore his hundred and twenty sheep per day making his days good ones. But this job did not tempt Jim.

Later, he became one of the regular workers on the station earning a pound a week, food and lodgings. He had left his family home for the homestead on the river. He had indelible memories of the walls of their small cottage; the memory of stories his father told him or he had read. In the hut, while his mates discussed the merits of the favourites for the Melbourne Cup and the pedigree of the twenty-three other horses that were to challenge the winner, Jim read.

During the day, when he was checking a paddock by himself or slowly riding behind a flock of sheep he was taking to the river to drink, his mind left the dust cloud surrounding him and went to a country white with snow with sleighs being drawn by horses with wind-blown manes. He would go from here to the large shady parks in the depths of which chateaux appeared like ghosts. Then, it was the sand of the hilly desert where monstrous statues and mutilated sphinxes were guarded by the pyramids. He thought also of the Orient of a Thousand and One Nights and he told himself that in order to see all these marvels, he would have to become rich. Yes, there was Western Australia where much gold had been found, but he had seen men coming from over there looking for work at the station and who were happy to find some.

Often on a Sunday, he would go to see his parents and each time he would re-read the walls. His entire childhood, his life's ambition was contained there. And he knew it.

CHAPTER IV

The sheep still seemed half asleep after their mid-day siesta. Their bleating could hardly be heard. Only the sound of their hoofs breaking twigs or dragging on dry leaves floated up in the dust cloud they made. They had been on the road for a week and the sheep had become pink; their shaved skin had quickly lost the whiteness of the newly-shorn and had greedily absorbed all the dust it possibly could. Their heads were down, their jaws were closed tight as they passed the blades of grass, their backs rolled together and gently shook like small lazy waves of a murky sea. This sea was made by three thousand five hundred sheep sold after the shearing season by *Lone Man Plain* at Coolapanda for twelve shillings and six pence a head. Coolapanda had marked each animal with a target – the station's brand – and a T (Travelling) that was compulsory for all sheep moving from one station to another over a distance of more than a few miles.

Syd was at the front of the flock with his dog and kept the head of the column almost in a straight line. Lou was on the left flank, Jim on the right and Macpherson, the head drover, was at the rear with his two dogs. The cook, who made up the staff and not the least of the people in the trail, had left before with his cart to choose a camp for the night where it would be easy to keep the sheep. A sixth member was always ahead by a day to alert the different owners of the paddocks they were going to go through, so they could have time to prevent their own sheep mingling with the herd passing through.

It was five o'clock when Dan, the cook, halted his horse and got down from his wagon. He unharnessed the animal and led it to the creek a couple of steps away to drink. Then he fettered it and left it to graze.

The drovers knew the spot. There was a fence at right angles to the creek, one part of it had been erected with branches and saplings. The creek, the fence and the hedge formed three sides of a square. Dan had been quick to cut down a few trees which he added to the fence where there were a few gaps appearing. He put up a fourth side using a piece of calico three feet wide and one hundred feet long held vertically by iron spikes he had pushed in eight feet apart.

With this work done, Dan got the sheep with its four legs tied up out of the wagon. It was destined to provide meat for the meal. Twenty minutes later, the slaughter finished, one of the legs was boiling in a petrol can on the fire.

He then filled two buckets with water, placed the billies on the fire and thought about washing himself beside the creek. He carefully brushed his hair that was still wet from washing and made a perfectly straight part down the middle of his skull.

Dan was not as dirty as half the cooks that one met here and there. He was even cleaner than a lot of them. His clothes were always noticed for their freshness. He seemed to spend any leisure he had either washing or fishing. But his cleaning methods were strangely inconsistent and showed that he lacked imagination sometimes. Otherwise he would never have boiled the leg of lamb in a petrol can that he had previously used to wash his clothes in.

When camped by the river, he always managed to find time to fish and catch a cat fish or a couple of Murray River cod for breakfast.

Dan had been a sailor for fifteen years. He had worked the stove on many boats and had thrown vegetable peelings overboard into the seven seas of four different oceans. He had been shipwrecked three times, once on the coast of New Zealand, once in the Black Sea and a third time near a small Polynesian island. This last experience made him lose interest in being a sailor. He had disembarked in Australia where he really hoped to see out his days. The only thing he didn't like about this country was that it was an island. Islands gave him the horrors. He rarely went to Sydney as he was afraid of being again tempted by that 'Great Blue Thing' – the ocean.

The sun was level with the plain when he heard the first bleatings of the sheep, followed by the air-born musketry of the whip lashes. The men had used their stockwhips to contain the sheep, but having smelt the creek water, they wanted to charge down to drink. The flock had to be halved allowing the first group to drink while keeping the others at a distance. When all the sheep had drunk, when the dogs had swum in the creek swallowing their weight in water, the men's shouts, the dogs barking and the cracking of the whips were all needed to make the herd go into the enclosure that had been prepared for them. The square formed by the creek, the iron wire fence, the barrier of branches and the long piece of calico had one opening where the sheep were driven through. Four stakes were placed equally in this gap and the dogs were tied up there. After wandering aimlessly around for a time, the sheep calmed down and remained almost quiet, some standing, others lying down. The head driver and his men watered their horses, unsaddled them and let them graze. Then, after going to the creek with their towels and soap, they sat near the fire and attacked the boiled leg of lamb.

They seemed to have forgotten the long day spent on the road between sunrise and sunset, behind a cloud of dust that moved forward ever so slowly.

Pushing a herd in front of you is probably the oldest job in the world – the first occupation taken up by man after living from hunting. He had felt superior when, with his intelligence, he had made a pointed spear to attack a wild animal with force. His second triumph had been the taming of defenceless, fearful animals living in groups. The length, the hazards and dangers of the hunt disappeared. The herd was still there and you only had to take a few steps to seize an animal and live off its flesh, to clothe yourself with its skin and wool. And for centuries to today, nations have preferred to remain shepherds minding their flocks while contemplating nature and dreaming.

Jim had asked to join the group. It was the first job he had had outside the station. He was intelligent and already knew how sheep behaved. By crossing the outer fence of *Lone Man Plain* he felt as though he entered into a world that was new to him. The Toorara paddocks strongly resembled those he was familiar with, but the grass and the trees already appeared different. He conscientiously set about doing his job. He got used to some of the energetic expressions the boss drover threw at the men who, half asleep in the sun, allowed the sheep to spread out a little across the plain or when the lead man went ahead too quickly. McPherson knew how much weight a sheep could lose on a day's march. He wanted to control the animals, give them time to graze without making them tired especially on the first few days. They needed to be gradually trained like soldiers in an army. The main drover, after inspecting the flock given to him, had rejected the ones that limped or were feeble. The sales contract gave him the right to refuse five per cent so he eliminated all the sheep that he thought were not ready for the long overland journey as well as the gummies, the ones with no front teeth since they could hardly benefit from the sparse dry grass in some of the districts.

Also the flock's tail wasn't long and there were few stragglers. Every now and then, an animal with set ideas refused to budge, no matter what, after lying down in the middle of the road. One man would pick it up from the ground, place it upright on its four feet, but the woolly 'mule' didn't want to know anything and was not at all interested in going on. It would then be thrown onto the neck of a horse until the next camp when Dan took it into his wagon. If a night's rest and reflection hadn't changed the sheep's disposition, that evening the cook gave it eternal peace – an efficient and painless death.

McPherson was born in Australia of Scottish parents and, like others from that country, he knew and understood the soul of the sheep. The Scot has no equal in raising sheep or cattle, but is not as interested in the horse leaving this honour to his neighbours the Irish. McPherson was proud of the flock he was pushing ahead as if he were the owner. "It's a good lot, of equal quality and not expensive", he kept repeating. In the evening when the tail began to slow down, he would drop his horse's bridle and jump down to seize one of the slow ones. In the blink of an eye, he would put it on its hindquarters, look at its teeth and then release the frightened animal by tapping its snout.

The boss drover was a man of few words, but what he said generally was worth the trouble of opening his mouth. He had read a lot and retained a lot. He was honesty itself and could never hide the disgust he felt when a man was too slippery and too clever in business. In fine company he knew his place, but he understood only the loyal struggle and, as soon as his adversary tried dishonest stuff, old Macpherson remained hard.

Dan and he had been together for several years on the New South Wales' roads. The drover liked the cook as much as the men did. Dan successfully made some cakes the Scot really liked. Syd and Lou were rolling stones who had no intention of gathering moss. Others worked for their livelihood which they considered was due to them. Nearly all their money helped quench a thirst – gambling. This thirst was stronger than any other. Since they were children they adored a game of chance. It started at the bush school where they had learned to read together, to bet with cards from cigarette packages before they had any money. Each had carefully raised a frilled-neck lizard and, on a miniature racecourse, won and lost numerous games until the day "Frilly", Syd's lizard, died suddenly crushed under the wheels of a buggy.

The two were still inseparable. They soon formed an association working on a station for a few months and, with the money earned, they bought camping material, rations, Belgium rifles, bullets and traps. They had only twenty-four rabbit skins the first week. But they soon knew how to set their traps better, covering the bascule with paper before hiding it under powdery earth. The traps were set in a line almost two kilometres long with an arrow traced in the soil and a hoe showing the direction to follow when they came carrying a lantern to retrieve them at night. They could hear the cries of their victims caught in the steel jaws. At times surprises awaited them: a trap had shut on one paw and the rabbit had escaped mutilated; further along an iguana the size of a crocodile had died, it's head caught. They got back to the camp with traps and rabbits in the middle of the night and fell onto their beds tired out and didn't wake up until the sun was high. They ate quickly and then had to skin a hundred to a hundred and fifty rabbits and bury their carcasses. They were too far from the rail line to sell the flesh. Skins paid well. But paddocks were quickly burnt and rabbits soon became wary and the men had to go further afield. After a few months, they were sickened by this job: the skinning of the animals surrounded by clouds of flies; the smell that impregnated their clothes and hands became intolerable. The pair decided on a change of air and occupation. For a week, Lou and Syd visited Sydney and the small capital they had was risked at several race courses, the bookies made the money though and the two friends left for the bush again without a penny, although persuaded they had enjoyed themselves immensely.

They gave up rabbiting and successively tried other jobs as rouseabouts in a shearing shed and as harvesters. The pay was good, but the work took up too much time and their love of money didn't go as far as neglecting their health or overtaxing their muscles. Again money earned was placed on race horses one festival day, but it happened that the horses they betted on were not winners.

Syd and Lou had gone back to work happy with their holidays and were now guarding the flock of sheep that was slowly going from *Lone Man Plain* to Coolapanda.

The men were on watch at night, each taking his turn since a broken branch, a rabbit passing or a fox going by could frighten the flock and make them break through the fence in panic and disperse in every direction. The guard kept the fire going, made himself some tea and smoked innumerable pipes to pass the time and keep awake. Jim, who was first on watch, often had a long conversation with Dan who went to bed late as he had to look after the bread in the oven for the next day. The oven was a large cast iron casserole with a lid that was completely covered with hot ashes. Jim loved to get the cook talking about his life as a wandering sailor. Dan always seemed ready to answer anything his mate wanted to know. What he knew of the countries he visited was rather succinct and gave the idea that he had studied the European areas much more than local ones. His impressions were vague and he spoke about them very briefly: Singapore hot as hell, but the pineapples are delicious and cost hardly anything. Japan was what he had seen on decorative fans. He had often met tigers and boa constrictors in Surabaya, Indonesia, but they were on his boat in cages going to Hamburg. He even remembered an escaped rhinoceros that had prevented the captain coming down the gangway for three hours.

He could have gone to see the pyramids, but it was really too hot that particular day; at Rio he wasted two hours haggling with the seller of fans, which were made of hummingbird feathers, and had no time to admire the bay. The first time they stopped at Aden, he went ashore to buy fresh vegetables and lettuce. They let him go and laughed heartily when he got back on board complaining that he hadn't seen a carrot top or cauliflower stalk. He found out only later that the people of Aden often came on board the visiting boats to get some green vegetables.

Dan continued as he lit his pipe again:

At Antofagasta [in northern Chile], I wasn't allowed to go on shore. I was told that if I managed to avoid getting two types of fever, chicken pox and another illness of the area that struck you down for six hours, I risked being knifed or getting a couple of bullets as I returned on board in the evening. This made my visit a lot more difficult so I stayed on board and fished, but the damned seals that hang around the port eat tons of fish and I didn't have any luck.

At Panama I took advantage of a few hours to buy a bowler hat. For a country known worldwide for its hats there wasn't much of a choice and the price was exorbitant. I paid four dollars fifty for one and it was made of very ordinary felt.

My third shipwreck made me give up sailing. It wasn't the actual shipwreck that frightened me so much; after all a shipwreck means one thing or another: either, you are saved, dry out and are called a lucky bugger, or you drown, you're finished, you don't even complain. This time I was still in my pyjamas in the water for a whole day with a life jacket somewhere off the coast of Fiji. I was found the next morning on a beach like a dead fish and with as much interest in living. Slowly after resting a little, I was able to stand. Fortunately, I found fresh water and ate some seashells that tasted of salt water. The second day after a lot of training and exercises, I managed to climb a palm tree and get some coconuts.

I didn't have anything with me. No, Jim, there were no cannibals on the island but I discovered worse than that – the stewardess of the second class passengers, a vixen who everybody on board feared and hated. She was in a small bay drying herself. She saw me first before I could hide.

I was young then otherwise I wouldn't have been able to put up with eighteen days alone in her company. She started by giving me orders as if we were on the ship and asking me to bring her food as if all that had to be done was to put a ladle in the broth and fill a cup. I quickly made her understand that half of the population on the island were socialists and communists and that each person had to work to live. I gave her coconuts and what I could of the sea food, but she had to work hard for her meals. She didn't give me an inch to move for she was afraid cannibals would come. I did my best to attract attention when a ship was seen passing, but it was only the fourth one that saw we were there.

This woman really hated me and the first thing she did when she got on board the boat which picked us up was to play me a foul turn. She told the captain that I had promised to marry her. I swore to the captain that I didn't have any such intention and, as she insisted, I begged the captain to put me back on the island. The good man knew I could be trusted.

The sheep continued on their path, accustomed now to the march of eight to ten miles covered each day at a pace that the men were rarely in the saddle, but walked along with an arm hooked in the bridle. The camps were fine. They could spend quiet nights even when the man on watch spent half an hour with his nose in his lap beside the fire he let go out. They hurried the sheep a little when they went by Merriwilloo for the owner of the station was known to be the most avaricious grump always keeping an eye on the sheep as they passed to make sure they didn't eat more grass than they needed. Old Tucker was as rich as Cresus. He lived like an Aborigine or almost, being happy with a miserable hut that was barely comfortable. He worked like two men and always had a small staff which he dragged the most he could from without paying more than another. And, in spite of all the stories that were told about his avarice and his harshness, he always found the workforce he wanted. The swagmen who passed by the station knew that the rations they got would only be a pinch of dust (flour) and a small amount of tea and sugar, never any meat. This economy cost old Tucker dearly one day – something like two hundred pounds sterling of fencing burnt in a bushfire started by a bottle knowingly left near a small pile of dry grass strewn with match candles.

They were going north. The country changed; dams and creeks were fewer. At Maltana, they passed a long line of camels led by Afghans, each animal was loaded with two bales of wool, a female camel was at the end carrying, in a calico bag, her young one too small for a long journey.

Jim watched this first vision of the Orient for a long time; the sun touching the earth, the silhouettes of this long line of camels didn't seem real, but a dream he had already had. The next day, he and his mates had another taste of the Orient: a sand storm reached them coming like a thick stream rolling across the plain leaving the sky clear above, a deep violet wall. They turned their backs against the blast which for a quarter of an hour was deafening. A few drops of rain fell, the air was freshened by rain in the distance and they could smell the delightful odour. Then the sky became serene, the air still and the flock continued in its halo of dust.

CHAPTER V

Two years later, Jim was riding across Bald Hill paddock one morning when he noticed the mailman coming, bone-shaken rhythmically on his horse and leading the grey speckled horse that carried bags filled with letters and newspapers. Jim halted his animal, cut some tobacco and filled his pipe: "What's new?" he shouted when the man was close.

After signalling 'hello' with a nod of his head, he said: "Pat Flannery beat Bill the sailor in eight rounds in Sydney. War has been declared between England and Germany." After a moment spent chasing the flies from his mount's left eye, he added: "I put a pound on Bill."

Jim, not being as much a sportsman as the mailman, had nothing to say about Flannery's win, but he asked for more detail about war being declared. The carrier of the news didn't know much more, so the two men went on their separate ways.

That evening, the workmen on *Lone Man Plain* station, about ten of them, commented on the news. Its importance had not yet struck these people who lived one hundred and twenty miles from any railway head and where the mail arrived only once a week.

Many thought of a German as a large person wearing a cap and glasses, his face covered by an enormous beard with a long pipe poking through. This is how they saw him stereotyped in the Sydney *Bulletin* and in the Melbourne *Punch*. Fred had known Germans in South Australia, farmers who worked as hard as beasts – all of them, men, women and children. They had beautifully organised properties. Jack had been employed for a year near Albury with vignerons who had astoundingly impressive vineyards.

A few remembered old Busch who, for many seasons, had sorted the wool on *Lone Man Plain*. The shearers and rouseabouts teased him and made him angry on purpose so he would mumble in German. And, when he found a belly carefully rolled up in the fleece on the table, Busch couldn't find enough words in the English language to express his resentment.

Harry knew a Pomeranian gardener in a New South Wales town who sometimes drank more than was good for him. Usually, he was calm and placid. One day, he caught the attention of police when he answered them in his mother tongue. He was thrown into prison while waiting for a hearing and had to pay a heavy fine the next day for rudely insulting the legal officers carrying out their duty.

In short, no one could throw a stone at the Germans. No one felt any hatred towards them then. But when the next mail brought news of the invasion of Belgium and they found out about the first atrocities of the war, feelings changed, except for a few.

"How does it affect me if Germany has declared war on England and the rest?" cried Short. "It doesn't give us any more or any less grass for the sheep and cattle. It won't increase our earnings, tobacco will be as expensive as before and beer at the Imperial will still cost six pence a glass. So what?"

"It's the grazier who will sell his sheep at a higher price," Williams added. "And the farmer will get more for his wheat. We don't give a toss about their war!"

Short continued: "If my grandfather left the old country behind in '68, it was probably because he had had enough of it. If he didn't go back, it was because he was happy in Australia. We don't give a bugger about their war!"

Hopkins, who had just come in, heard Short's last tirade. "What would you do, Short, if you saw me kicking little Sam Robinson?"

"I'd give you one in the eye," replied a red-faced Short.

"Why?" asked Hopkins. "The kid's not yours... Let me finish and don't get worked up about it. Germany is kicking tiny Belgium to death. I'm not Belgian, but because of this I'm off tomorrow to enlist. I'm breaking a contract that would bring me money, but I don't care. I like it here, Short, but I'm leaving tomorrow. My father came to Australia quite young. He had his reasons for coming to the colonies, but he has never forgotten the old country and has always spoken of it at home so that I wouldn't forget it existed."

"If you want to go and get your face smashed," said Williams after a long silence, "go, you're free."

"We won't be doing anything bad by getting our faces smashed," Hopkins continued, "and it's possible that *Lone Man* will be well represented there. There will certainly be some who attach a high price to their face. And there are Blacks who won't understand why we go twelve thousand miles to fight. But there will be a good number embarking, God willing!"

Jim was one of the men who left.

Lone Man Plain was his and his parents' whole world. The small garden with the passionfruit vine that sheltered the veranda from the afternoon sun, the magical carpet that was already yellowed from the smoke of the open fireplace – this was his home, his most valued place. Now that he was about to leave to go to the other side of the world, now that the deeply desired moment he had dreamt about had come, he thought the price to pay would be a heavy one. He had to give up his entire past! He knew there was something else, a voice told him to go and fight there with the others and the voice didn't have to say it twice. When he said to his parents, "I'm going", his father answered: "My boy, I'm pleased you spoke first." His mother cried, but quickly wiped away her tears as she embraced him. Then, he felt as if everything was spinning around him. He had a strange emptiness in his chest, as if all his innards had been removed. Nothing could get him to eat his evening meal.

After the farewells, he left the cottage and didn't turn in his saddle for he knew they were on the veranda watching. He waved his hat two or three times, he spurred his horse on and galloped to the top of the hill and descended at the same speed disappearing from sight as quickly as possible. Then he allowed Tall Boy to walk and caressed his neck as if to apologise for having spurred him on so much. It seemed his horse understood and forgave him.

He shook hands with the boss and his wife, who wished him luck, and left the station. He turned around on horseback to look at the white roofs that made patches among the dark green of the orange trees and the graceful feathery leaves of the pear trees. He felt his eyes mist up as he watched the homestead grow smaller in the distance and an anxiety clenched his entire being. Before crossing the creek with its curtain of trees which would hide the station from sight, he made another about-turn and found himself in full sunlight. Standing up on his stirrups, he waved goodbye to his parents, the people he lived with and everything that was around them, everything that was *Lone Man Plain*, its grey soil, its flocks of sheep and the pale blue sky. He opened his mouth but no sound came out – his throat was so constricted.

Crossing the creek that came up to his horse's girth, he bent down, took some water in the hollow of his hand and drank. He felt an urgent need to touch everything around him, everything that was familiar to him. He tore off some gum leaves as he went by, rubbed them in his hand and took deep breaths of the volatile essence they gave out. He followed attentively the cloud of noisy cockatoos as if he hadn't seen this every day of his life. A flock of ewes fled before him. Instinctively, he whistled his dog, forgetting he had left him in his father's care.

After a two-day ride, he finally arrived at the town where he was to catch the train for Sydney. He had one more emotion to overcome. He went to the stables to say goodbye to his horse which the mailman had promised to take back to *Lone Man Plain*. As the chestnut ate the bread and sugar he had brought with him, Jim patted and praised him. He tried to convince himself that the animal didn't know what was happening, but there was a persistent fear that he noticed a sad look in Tall Boy's deep blue eyes. He staggered out of the stables holding in his left hand some hair he had just cut from his mane.

After spending an entire day aboard the train, Jim arrived in Sydney exhausted, famished and very thirsty. He went quickly from one office to another, was examined by the medical officer and, after three days, was assigned to a small group of the Australian Imperial Force with a four-digit number.

Serious training began once in camp: camping in a tent was nothing to men of the bush, but they were less enthusiastic when required to learn the very first thing their mothers had taught them – to walk. The Australian of the Great Plains is a horseman. He always tries to find a way to do the minimum walking. He doesn't hesitate to saddle a horse in search of another one he can see five hundred yards away. In some small towns, the lamp-lighter was on horseback as well as the town crier, or the postman who delivered telegrams.

Discipline is a word that an Australian finds disagreeable. It's something he hardly knows. In a country where every necessity is easily procured and where excess is not rare, a land of plenty for the worker makes men rather aggressively independent. In a country that has the highest record of industrial strikes, that is 695 in two years (with 507 in New South Wales), military discipline is a process that takes a long time to blossom.

Once in khaki uniform, the average Australian must get it in his head that he has a superior officer and that he has to salute his superior each time he passes him in the street. Up until now even his boss was not particularly considered his superior and when the boss didn't please, the man simply left and went elsewhere. It was quite simple. The idea was new for some, not to be able to advise the captain to look for another man to do the job. But they got used to the idea for there was no alternative. There were some unhappy with their superiors who left the Sydney camp and, using another name, offered their services in another colony, Victoria or Tasmania. They had not deserted. They changed regiment. In England, saluting is not as common as in France otherwise you would catch cold too often. In Australia, they salute less than in England as sunstroke is too dangerous. Moreover, a salute is a sign of respect and the Australian, who has a lot of good qualities, doesn't have a well developed sense of respect. It is probably not his fault. In a new country, there is only age or beauty that commands respect.

Despite this, after a few weeks of military life, the men had the appearance of soldiers with their chinstrap always in place. Their walk had changed slightly; they no longer looked as if they had just got off a horse for they had done a lot of marching and drilling.

After two months of camp life, the moment to embark arrived. The triumphant ranks of men marched through the town between two rows of people waving handkerchiefs and throwing flowers. The large transport boat left the pier amid great enthusiasm.

Leaning on the rail, Jim kept his eyes for a long time on the wharf dark with crowds of people. At the signal of departure, he saw the side of the boat leave the pier's tar-covered skeleton. The space of a few inches held by the wharf's collision buffers suddenly increased. Jim calculated for thirty seconds that he could still jump onto the wharf. A few feet below, it was already an abyss and now the seemingly smaller crowd were still waving handkerchiefs that resembled a flight of seagulls.

He then sensed the moment, like pain inflicted by the blade of a cold knife. His two hands tightened as they clutched the large teak ramp and two tears flowed, small, like those of a man who rarely cried.

There were two thousand five hundred men squashed aboard the transport ship. After passing the Great Australian Bight and, when those suffering from seasickness got back on deck, they quickly became used to life at sea. Every morning, they had limbering up exercises, technical theory and lectures. The remaining time, they were able to enjoy being relatively idle, although it was varied with all types of sporting activities.

CHAPTER VI

They had good weather. The fleet, made up of thirty-eight troop transport ships protected by five escort ships, advanced in rows of four. There were about twenty thousand men, Australians, Tasmanians and New Zealanders. This armada coming from the Antipodes was strangely grand. It was an expedition never seen before, an army of peaceful people who had never felt the strong arm of the invader, an army that didn't know hate, who joined together voluntarily to be in the bloodiest war in History.

They were a mixture of all social classes, from the bank clerk from Brisbane or Townsville to the stockman from the large stations of the interior. The miner from Cloncurry and New Guinea, the pearl diver from Western Australia, the plantation worker from the New Hebrides, the shearer from the Riverina, the sugar-cane cutter from Burdekin, the opal miner from Lightning Ridge, the seeker of sapphires from Emma-ville – all had answered the call. Enthusiastic and generous daredevils, they were indeed the grandchildren of adventurous pioneers who, more than a century before, had made the opposite journey to try their fortune in the large islands of the Pacific.

They crossed the equator with its grotesque and unchangeable traditional ceremonies. And soon after at night, they noticed for the first time the Great Bear without losing sight of the Southern Cross, the cherished constellation they had chosen for their flag.

"That's the Great Bear," said Pat Malloy who was by trade a dingo hunter. "Honestly, you have to have a good imagination to see a bear, or any other animal, male or female! No, it doesn't have the suaveness of our Southern Cross, does it, Gus?"

With his pipe between his teeth, Gus barely moved his lips to say: "Not by half." But beside this sudden expression of a very set opinion, astronomy didn't seem to interest him much.

When they were in sight of the Suez Canal, they recognised the pink sand and the copper-coloured sky they had often seen in pictures, but they had always thought they were the work of artists who were not very conscientious in portraying reality. With Port Said in view, the order came that no one was to disembark. Of course, there were some members of the expedition who were anxious to feel solid earth beneath their feet and about a hundred men dived overboard and swam to shore. Some were stopped; others rejoined their battalions in Cairo after their brief absence without leave.

Once on Egyptian soil, Jim and his mates camped at the foot of the Pyramids on the same area occupied by Napoleon's army. These young men from the youngest civilisation in the world looked first with admiration at these gigantic monuments in the middle of the desert without understanding how they got there.

Generally, the Australian is a practical-minded person: he admires what is beautiful, but considers the practical value of what he sees. A king has a mountain built with bricks so that his name will be remembered in History. This is a pro-American claim whose significance he does not understand. He better understands structures like the Aswan Dam built in drought country. He would like to have a lot more like it in Australia. He does, however, admire the Pyramids simply because he is able to assess roughly the gigantic work effort they represent and the energy used by an army of labourers, difficulties overcome using slow, painful means of transport, along with the primitive systems of levers and pulleys .

A few hundred yards from the Great Pyramid, Sergeant Ted Burton was emptying sand from his left sock, a task he couldn't do without calling the venerable land of the Pharaohs "this rotten country". Burton was one of the most determined champions of the Australian Labor Party. He had been one of the most militant members of the Organized Workmen's League (OWL), a union whose ideal was a three-hour day, never piecework and to be paid one pound sterling a day. Ted was never satisfied. He groaned continually. If ever he gets to Heaven, he will probably groan because Saint Peter will ask him for his pass. Despite this, in spite of his political opinions, Ted Burton had enlisted at the first call without asking if the work was by the hour or by the task. Away from meeting rooms, he was a model citizen soldier and soft as a lamb.

He was given the rank of Sergeant and had under him Private MacIntyre ("Mac" as he was called) whose sheep he had shorn two consecutive seasons. Mac's father owned six pastoral stations in New South Wales and had underhand dealings with sheep on a large scale. Everyone knew that, after breakfast one morning in the Hotel Australia in Sydney, he had purchased thirty-five thousand sheep he had never set eyes on and had resold them five minutes before lunch for a profit. Calculations were made with a pencil on his left sleeve and the transaction concluded with his buyer with two Martini cocktails, with a cherry in the bottom of each glass.

Young Mac wanted to enlist no matter what as an ordinary soldier and had refused the rank of Second Lieutenant he could have legitimately had. Ted Burton thought this refusal worthy of his secret approval.

"Well Ted", asked Mac, "what do you think of the Pyramids?"

"It's true they make a great pile of stones," said Ted. "They say it took thousands of men and years to build them. It proves that time and workers were not worth much in those days. Still there must have been some strikes?"

"Nothing doing like that," said Mac, with a twinkle in his eye. "These people didn't have syndicates or unions. And they weren't paid. Just given food and the whip!"

"So they were slaves?"

"Probably."

"That's really disgusting!" said Ted. "And all this work was done to shelter kings and queens who were preserved and covered in calico, like hams and dried like apricots from Mildura!"

"Your union," said Mac, "doesn't want to allow coloured people to work in Australia. What would you do if I imported some tame monkeys to pick fruit at home? The Egyptians put monkeys on different jobs. It seems that during banquets, monkeys were torchbearers. I reckon that this cheap work would become really expensive when the torch-bearing monkeys began fighting and continued into the banquet room!"

"It's funny the way they write using images," Ted went on.

"When you write to your girlfriend, what do you put below the last line?"

"That's my business", replied Ted abruptly.

"Yes, I know," said Mac smiling. "I simply want to show that you also use hieroglyphics when you put crosses for kisses at the bottom of your letters. It's the same thing when you see a sheep with a crescent shape on its left shoulder, you know straightaway that it's an animal belonging to Moolana."

Ted didn't answer. He could scarcely answer for he was busy cleaning his pipe with a piece of wire he had taken from a soda bottle. Jim, who was sitting near them and had been listening for a while, timidly joined in the conversation a little like he would enter a room on tippy toes.

"I reckon that in Australia we have the record for heat and flies. But I can already see that Egypt can show us something beside her monuments! I have known this country ever since I could see and imagine.

I have seen it and have imagined it in our cottage at *Lone Man Plain*. I have dreamt of it day and night and now that I can walk on its sand and see the Sphinx and the Pyramids, I confess that they are much more grandiose than in all my dreams. Ted finds it difficult to understand the usefulness of these piles of stones. But if they only make us think of their age, more than four thousand years old, it's something we will never forget. Our country is scarcely a hundred year-old civilisation, although it is one of the oldest countries in the world."

Ted was still cleaning his pipe. Mac was next to speak: "It could be said that the Gods and the Devils, especially the Devils, got it into their heads to play a game that would mystify the entire earth. Indians came down from the Himalayas, crossed the valleys and the seas and are now in Flanders. Arabs from the Sahara are in the north of France. There are even redskins in khaki fighting in the surrounding areas. Us from the Antipodes – Australians, New Zealanders, Maoris, Fijians, island folk from Norfolk Island or Samoa – here we are in Egypt as old as the world itself! We don't believe in ghosts, but this sand makes them rise like the vapours of a mirage. Kings, slaves, endless armies, Bonaparte and his soldiers, so many ghosts surround us!"

"I would really like to walk through Cairo," said Ted after taking a last puff of his pipe. "The living interest me more, although I hate all the dirty negroes. These damned darkies earn eight pence a day, they live well and also find the means to buy stuff to smoke and they don't even work every day!"

"Ah! Ted," said Mac slapping his thigh, "I was waiting for you there! These 'dirty negroes' have the ideal your OWL is looking for, that is to easily earn enough to live on by working the least number of hours possible. These people can do that for they don't have many needs. But for you, your needs increase the more you earn, you try to climb an escalator backwards and naturally you are never happy! If you want to live without harming the palms of your hands, go to an island in the Pacific, but be prepared to eat cooked bananas, yams and coconuts washed with delicious clear water. When we travel we sometimes treat Blacks as bone idle as if we wouldn't do the same if we were not forced to work!"

"Go on!" said Ted. "A day will soon come when the government will give each of us a piece of land, a small house and a cow."

"Yes," said Mac, "and the next day your neighbour will have drunk away his house and cow and will want to share your cow and your house with you!"

"Ah, no!" said Ted. "I'll keep what is mine! ..."

"It's always like that, the owner kills the socialist, it doesn't take long!"

"Jim," Mac suddenly shouted, "isn't it rather disgusting to talk about these things here? Look at the full moon coming up behind that dune. Isn't it beautiful? Let's go and see the Pyramids in the moonlight. Are you coming, Ted?"

"No," said Ted. "I've seen your Pyramid. I'm sick and tired of it. I've bought coloured postcards and that's enough for me!"

Mac and Jim walked a few hundred yards in the sand to the foot of the Great Pyramid.

After a long silence, Jim was the first to speak. "I wonder if these kings, by building these monuments which were to keep their names for posterity and to prove how great and powerful they were, did not prove to the contrary, the minuscule smallness of everything that is human, even that which is royal! In the imagination, this million-ton mountain crushes, pulverises these few pounds of desiccated objects that are the royal mummies. And in spite of everything, we came and upset them in their impregnable fortresses. Some are in museums covered in glass containers labelled and marked: 'Do not lean on the glass'. What a contrast between the Pyramid and the display box!"

The moon rose in the sky lighting up one side of the Pyramid and leaving in its shadow the second visible side. The two men walked further away. The overpowering closeness prevented them judging the silvery blue light. They remained silent for a long time. Mac suddenly said: "We leave tomorrow for the peninsula. It seems that this is the last night before the battle. The moon is there in all its splendour telling us to use our eyes fully, and think hard with every fibre of our being, to admire with complete reverence what we can. What is in store for us? Even the Sphinx can't answer this question. We didn't know each other Jim, before getting the ship that brought us here. We knew each other on board and we shared a tent in camp and tomorrow we will be mates at arms. I think this evening we are a bit more than that. This night – Cleopatra must have seen many like us – brings us closer together for we are both here probably for the last time and we won't ever forget these last hours in Egypt, because they are all that is left of our youth ... Jim, we don't know if the old Europe will keep us as she has kept others, as she will keep even more. We knew these were the stakes when we left. If you are lucky and get back, and if I stay here, would you take a letter for me to Sydney to my family ... and as for me, if I can do something for you? Chances are equal..."

"Thank you," said Jim. "I'll write a few words tonight, you never know! I don't have any feelings either way. There are thousands of us in the same boat. Look again at the pyramid. It will go on being warmed by the sun and cooled by the moon for centuries to come unless the Germans come here. Next to these monuments, we can clearly see what we are – grains of sand that swirl around its base. We are no more than that and our existence has, in the universe, as much importance as these damn flies that pester us in their myriads."

They walked slowly back to camp. Then before going to bed, they exchanged sealed envelopes without saying a word and firmly shook hands for the first time.

The next day, they embarked for Lemnos from where, after three days, they left for the peninsula. They disembarked between 4.30 and 5.00 in the morning and, as soon as they were on land, they could hear heavy shells exploding on the beach and its surrounds and the men knew the hour of their baptism had come. They got busy doing what those who went before them had done and they hollowed out dugouts in the hills facing the sea.

Then there were the days spent in the trenches where they returned carrying the equipment of a mate who had been brought down by a Turkish sniper, or carrying a wounded man. There were the baths in the sea that were often interrupted by bombs falling onto the beach or that made geysers in the water. In the midst of these daily horrors that they got used to after a short time, they couldn't help smiling at some things that happened, as if to throw a little humour on the entire nightmare.

There was Enry Wood who came back from the trenches like a condemned man, walking anxiously and comically at the same time as if he had just unsuspectedly sat on a lit stove. It wasn't long after that he got out of the ambulance having been made lighter by the doctor extracting eleven gramophone needles from his body. This new type of Turkish grenade deserved the nickname of "prickly" [*pelote*] which he accepted most gracefully.

There was tall Simpson from North Queensland whose left arm they had seen taken off by an exploding bomb. A mate had tied it as best he could and was going to go with him to the help post when Simpson went back the way he came despite his mate's pleas who was more terrified than he was of his wound.

"I want to find my arm," yelled Simpson as he began searching around. "Your bloody arm?" asked his mate. It's not's worth a thing, so leave it! You're going to get shot."

"My arm's worth nothing?" Simpson retorted. "By golly! And my watch!"

Simpson found his arm with his watch intact and a little later this made him one of the happiest and healthiest of one-armed men.

Sergeant Ted Burton lost two of his men. Mac fell the third day, dying two hours after without any pain or a single complaint and as if he had known that his happy youthful life had been merely on loan. He seemed ready to give it back at the first sign.

And Burton, the socialist striker and enemy of all bosses, said that same evening to those who were near him in the dugout: "*Well, Mac was a white man!*" And he blew his nose hard using two fingers because his handkerchief was wrapped around his left hand which was bleeding.

Two days later, a bomb exploded near Jim. Jim covered his eyes with his hand and knew he was blind.

CHAPTER VII

The two stretchers followed each other, being slowly and gently carried by their caring bearers. Dick was on the second one; his face was white and his right sleeve was limp and covered in large blotches of blood that became darker in the sun and air.

"Give me a cigarette and light it for me," muttered Dick to the stretcher-bearers. But it fell on deaf ears. Dick wanted his cigarette and when Dick wanted something he generally was able to get it. He swore when he asked for the third time. The Royal Australian Medical Corps men bent and gently placed the stretcher on the ground. One of them took a packet of Woodbines from his pocket, took out a cigarette, lit it and gave it to the man who thanked him almost without opening his teeth.

Jim, then Dick were looked at by the doctors and ended up in beds next to one another on a hospital ship. Jim had his eyes covered with a thick bandage and Dick had had his right arm completely blown off by an exploding bomb. Their first chat took place when they were suffering the usual fever that follows such serious wounds, as if it was just a hint of pain. A few words were directed at the ceiling, because life seemed too heavy and the body too tired to turn sideways.

"How's things?" asked one of them.

"Not too bad," the other grimaced.

"Where did you get it?"

"Where my eyes were."

"Damned bad luck," said the one-armed man.

"It could have been worse," replied the man with his eyes bandaged.

And Dick seemed suddenly to forget the burning below his shoulder and closed his pale lips over clenched teeth to stop himself speaking. And in his heart, in his poor head, his unspoken words resounded like a loud cry in the vault of a cave: "Blind! Poor Bugger!"

From that moment, he felt for his suffering mate something like a deep love for an older brother, as if he needed him to come and help him, to try everything possible to make his night less dark.

"You're not certain you've lost your sight. Even the doctors don't always know."

"No mistake this time old chap. It's better to know the worst from the start."

Dick, who had lived for years by himself in a bush camp spending weeks without speaking two sentences, astonished himself by becoming almost loquacious. Sometimes, he stopped in the middle of a story to ask his bed-mate: "Are you asleep? I'll stop talking, if it annoys you."

Jim said to continue and began to break his own silence. Poor Dick could hardly speak of anything but the bush and what took up most in his life – his father. His father had argued with his own family one day and left England for Australia with a few pounds in his pocket. He knew no one in the Antipodes. He didn't have the time, nor did he think to obtain a few letters of introduction.

The day after he got off ship in Sydney, he began looking for any type of work. Chance helped and took him to the door of an employment agent who placed station workers, teachers, gardeners, rabbit-poisoners, cooks (both male and female) – in fact, all those who wanted some type of job. The waiting room was bursting with women who exchanged their views on the places they had just left, the quality of certain types of stoves and the faults of their respective husbands. Because of this program, a man could wait for half an hour in the visiting room of the *Work Providing Agency.* The agent had him enter his tiny office and asked him the type of work he would like.

Accountant? The employment agency had just the thing, not in Sydney, but on a station called Gooratoola Downs, a ten-hour train journey and a full day in a coach away in the country. The agent rose and pointed out a spot on the map in the north-west corner of New South Wales where the names of towns were very scattered. "They want an accountant storeman for thirty shillings a week, accommodation and food included, and travel expenses paid for if the accountant stays for six months or more."

The new-arrival filled in two sheets the agent gave him and signed them: John Bernard Jerry.

The agent asked a few questions. He knew he was dealing with a new chum and believed he could send him to Gooratoola Downs without obtaining information about the future accountant. He promised to send a telegram to the station announcing his arrival. Without a murmur, Bernard paid the agent the fifteen shillings commission.

The trip was long and tiring. At six in the morning after a solid breakfast, he got the stagecoach, which looked a lot like Cinderella's carriage, which would have been in use for more than a hundred years. A man on horseback galloped ahead of the four horses for the coach had to go through thirty-five gates that he had to open and close.

On a beautiful sunny morning, Bernard saw the Australian bush for the first time. The magpies' song was the thing that struck him most and it still remained the freshest of his first impressions. The road with very few travellers on it crossed a large plain where solitary trees, or sometimes a few together, grew here and there. The absence of hedges and bushes gave the plain the impression of a gigantic park. The defined smooth trunks of the eucalypts seemed to belong to carefully pruned trees.

Ben, the coachman, took Bernard under his wing and set about giving him a series of the most edifying talks about flora and fauna and all sorts of things Australian. Ben knew this area well as he had been travelling it every day, apart from Sundays, for almost six years. He covered sixty miles daily with three sets of horses.

Now and then, he would stop in front of a mud-slab hut that acted as a hotel, or a cabin which was a post office. There were trees that had boxes nailed on their trunks, from these a bunch of letters and newspapers would be collected and another bundle would then take their place. At midday, he stopped at a small cottage to water and feed the horses and have a meal of salted beef and bread and drink very strong sugary tea. An hour before sunset, the coach went through the Gooratoola gate where Bernard found a buggy waiting for him to take him to the station homestead.

He stayed two years on the station. He would not have left if he hadn't married the schoolteacher hired there to teach the boss's children. She was a young English woman who, like him, had left her home in spite of herself. The dark orange trees in the garden had suspected from the start that something would happen as their shade had protected, more than once, the two exiled young people when they were talking together about the "old country".

Bernard and his wife gathered together their small savings and bought a horse and cart and some goods which they intended to sell as they travelled through the bush. The boss at Gooratoola had offered the young couple two horses and harnesses in demonstration of the esteem and affection he held for the teacher and his accountant.

For them, life was idyllic. They travelled the countryside, stopping at stations where they always found food for their horses and buyers of their merchandise. Sometimes, they camped beside the river erecting a small tent on the side of their carriage and fished. The teacher quickly learnt the secrets of this gypsy lifestyle. She could light a fire in the rain and the wind; make bread in the ashes; cut meat bought at a station, cook with very few utensils and harness the horses.

Life didn't seem much more complicated when their son Dick was born in a tiny town somewhere in the north of New South Wales, beside a river that rarely had enough water flowing for two consecutive months. Dick's birth was not the only reason Blandora township was well known. Its celebrity was unusual, but it didn't last. Every stranger coming to Blandora was offered one pound sterling if they could throw a stone from one side of the river to the other. But there were no stones, not the least little pebble within a ten-mile radius. One day Blandora had to pay the money they had been unwisely offering for such a long time. A traveller, who had known about this, came with stones in his pocket. Blandora's celebrity collapsed, just as Goliath had, by a single stone. The story goes on to say that the stranger was magnanimous by spending the pound sterling he had earned at the only hotel in the area and the whole of the Blandora adult population got royally drunk at his expense.

Dick was eight years old when his mother died. Bernard found the bush a very solitary place after losing his companion, but he knew he had to raise the young boy. Fortunately, camp life had made him into a solid youngster who already knew how to play his part in life helping his father every day with various tasks.

He received a rudimentary but practical education. His mother had taught him to read, write and count and, every evening by the campfire after studying from the few books he had, the child listened to stories his father told him of the "old country". Early on, Dick became interested in the small island called England on the other side of the globe.

He knew by heart the description of a large house in a vast park with rows of trees which no one now knew how old they were; trees that were different from the eucalypts and which lost their leaves every year, remaining bare throughout the winter when the house and the park disappeared under a huge white layer as if bags of flour had been shaken over the country. It was snow which was very cold and burnt your hands if you touched it for too long – a strange thing that melted when touched, but which became hard when it was pressed together. At the back of the park, the lake was frozen and you could walk and slide over the water.

The child could not imagine a Christmas in snow that froze and burnt your hands, when days were so short and it was dark by four o'clock. The Christmases he knew were long, hot days with flies and mosquitoes tormenting men and animals.

The park's entrance was a large iron gate. Dick had difficulty understanding why the gate was shut at night to stop people going in. You couldn't camp in the park, or let the horses loose there so they could graze, as was the practice in Australia. The pylons that supported the gate were surmounted by griffons, animals that always had their mouths open and their claws ready to strike. Each griffon held a shield in one of its paws on which there were two crescents and the head of a wild boar.

Bernard had to answer the child's numerous questions: yes, there were sheep, cows and horses in the park. There were also pheasants like fat hens with long tails. There were rabbits. A man went through the park to prevent people killing the pheasants and rabbits. And from time to time, friends came with guns and killed everything that had feathers and fur.

Dick thought the ideas people had over there in the "old country" were strange.

The house itself was very old. It had been partially rebuilt several times, but the kitchen and the dining room were more than three hundred years old. The dining room was haunted and Dick learnt about ghosts: dead people who were reborn to frighten the living.

One evening when the clouds quickly covered the moon, hiding it for a few minutes then leaving it to flood the plain and the trees, Bernard told Dick the dramatic story that had taken place in the old mansion in England many long years ago. It was a story of a knight and his son.

One day when the two of them, armed from head to toe, were leaving for war, the knight once again asked his son to marry the woman who had been chosen for him.

The son then drew his sword from its scabbard and said defiantly: 'I swear by this brilliant straight blade like a ray of sunshine, by all the fibres of this steel, pure and blue as the moon, that I will only marry the woman of my own choosing.'

So the knight in anger brandished his sword in reply. The son saw the weapon raised towards him. He didn't move nor did his arm make the slightest movement to block the blow that sliced through his helmet as if it were a ripe piece of fruit and struck him dead at his father's feet.

Dick wanted to ask many more questions, but he didn't dare. His father had told this story in a tone that was different from his normal voice. He soon knew it by heart, imitating to perfection the voice his father used to tell the story.

Iron-clad knights had haunted his imagination. He had often looked for them in the shade of the trunks of the eucalypts, but they never revealed themselves. One summer evening, he amused his father by saying that Australia was a country too hot for knights encased in their armour. They would never be able to fight! And Bernard agreed that Australia was not particularly suitable for them. The idea suddenly came to him of a knight trying to chase a fly that had got in through the holes in his visor, or suddenly feeling a bull dog ant climbing up his leg under the steel puttee.

Bernard had often spoken to Dick about the school he had attended. It was a large school where football, cricket and many other things were played. There were about six hundred pupils and they were always hungry, because they were never given enough to eat. The refectory was huge with a very high ceiling and large portraits covered the walls – a dining room for a king in which you always went hungry.

Later, Dick understood that his father and his grandfather had had a quarrel resulting in dividing the land between them. Bernard never said why he had left the large house and the large park where he grew up. The child had too much faith in his father to believe for a single moment that he had committed an unforgiveable mistake. And instinctively he blamed the grandfather he didn't know, but Bernard had never said a bad word against him.

*

A poor season stopped their wanderings. Grass was rare and fodder was so expensive that Bernard had to sell the horses and then the wagon a short time after. They set up camp on a station where father and son found work for five months throughout the drought. One morning, not long after this difficult season, Bernard died as he was waking up – suddenly, before anything could be done for him.

Dick went back to camping alone, catching possums and rabbits for four years. He lived by himself with the memory of his father whose presence he often felt, as he sat near the fire that was his only nightly companion. Once a week, he went to the closest store to sell the rabbit and possum skins he had gathered. He exchanged a few words with a few people, purchased what he needed and went back to his camp.

As soon as he heard that the war had begun, he folded his tent, sold his dogs or gave them away and headed for Sydney to enlist.

And now a ship, painted white with large red crosses on its sides and lit up at night by hundreds of electric lights as if ready for a Venetian carnival, was taking him and Jim to a country that had haunted their young dreams.

CHAPTER VIII

Five o'clock. It was already dark. Dick sat watching by pulling back the blind in the train compartment that was lowered under orders because of the zeppelins. A bluish fog like a pale-inky mist was everywhere. As the train passed, he could see the lights of houses making what looked like luminous oil spots on their drawn curtains.

He was vaguely able to make out what seemed to be a sea of roofs that he guessed was immense. A multitude of chimney pots reminded him of a forest of pine trees cut-down to three feet from their base. At times, his eye dived over deep and sombre streets that appeared to him like canyons.

The train travelled slowly; then stopped at the burst of a small bomb. There was a groan, then a sound like an avalanche. It was another train going in the opposite direction. Dick heard shouts and singing. It was the blokes going to the Front in France on a troop train. There were still more, thank God, to replace those missing or dead, to carry on there where others had fallen.

The train started again. Suddenly a voice shouted in the compartment: "London! Hey guys! we're not dreaming, we're not drunk, it really is London!"

Those that were suffering the least and not in so much pain shouted three times: "Hip! Hip! Hoorah!" And 'cooees' came from everywhere on the crowded train.

Then one cooee, louder than the others, resounded – separately. It was Jim. Steve Barrett, who lost a leg at Pine Hill, said in a voice that was happy, yet tinged with pity: "Good old Jim!"

"I'll not see the old country again," said Jim, "but I will march on this earth where our fathers and grandfathers came from... Good old England!" After a moment he continued: "Where are the men who spoke about cutting the ties that bind us to old England? By God, we have shown that we can give our skins for her when she needs us, more than our skin... *I*'ve given two blue eyes!"

"Three cheers for England!" someone shouted.

The last hurrah was still in the air when the train came into the gigantic smoky cavern of Waterloo Station. Red Cross vehicles were lined up, bumper to bumper, at the wharf and even at the station scarcely twelve feet from the train carriages. Volunteer stretcher-bearers in blue uniforms were lined up ready to transfer the wounded to hospital.

Dick got out unassisted – one of the first of the walking wounded – half dazed by the pale pink electric lamps that dazzled every now and then and which seemed, in the London fog, to be another luminous fog. Three stretchers went into each ambulance. Dick took charge of Jim and guided him to the inside seat of the ambulance beside the nurse.

The vehicle drove between two clusters of people who were greeting them, waving and throwing flowers. They were mainly women and Dick gallantly blew them kisses. The nurse gathered up the flowers from the floor and gave them to the wounded men. She put a handful between Jim's hands and he stayed for a long time with his face buried in the roses, breathing in their perfume and kissing them. "Roses! they're red aren't they, nurse?" he asked.

"Yes, deep red," she replied.

"Hmm," said Jim proudly, "I can still recognise roses. Dick, hand me a cigarette."

The nurse had some in her apron pocket. She took one, lit it and put it in Jim's hand.

"Thank you," said the blind man. "Are you English, Nurse?

"Yes."

"Will you tell me what we are passing?"

"We are now crossing the Thames on Westminster Bridge."

"Are there boats on the river?"

"You can't see anything at the moment. There's so little light because of the zeppelins. We are passing in front of the Parliament, a tall square tower with a clock, a little further on is Westminster Abbey; your hospital is quite close by. When I have a free day, I'll come for you and we'll go wherever you wish. What's your name?"

"Jim Clarke from *Lone Man Plain* in New South Wales. What's your name, Miss?"

"Nurse Joan."

The blind man searched for the nurse's hand and squeezed saying: "Thank you Nurse Joan for your kindness."

During this time Dick looked at the nurse's face each time she turned her head towards him and he thought she was beautiful in her white headgear. The electric light that lit up the inside of the ambulance made it possible for him to see she had beautiful hair.

Dick was bold enough to ask her if a bed could be chosen near his mate Jim and Nurse Joan said that, if it were possible, she would.

The next morning for one long minute, Dick looked at Jim in the bed to his right with his face half-hidden by thick bandages. The almost absolute immobility of his body made him think his mate was still sleeping. Then by lifting himself slightly, he noticed that the fingers of the right hand on top of the blanket were moving. Starting with the thumb, they moved straight up. Dick guessed the blind man was counting.

"That's four what?" asked Dick.

"Four weeks of darkness, old man. Did you sleep well?"

"Yes indeed. What about you?"

"Like an old shoe ... My pain has almost gone."

"Mine too. It's the London air, I'm sure."

"What's the weather like?" asked Jim.

"A bit of sunshine," said Dick, noticing a thick ray that looked like a long strip of fresh pine tree slanting against one of the window panes.

After a short silence, Jim said without raising his voice much: "Say, the nurse who was in the ambulance last night, is she nice? I'm sure she is, she has a sweet voice. She must have beautiful eyes. Eyes are generally beautiful when they are lit by goodness."

"Old man," said Dick, "you haven't lost your judgement. Nurse Joan is just as you say; she struck me as soon as I saw her. I have to say that we haven't seen a lot of beautiful women for weeks. The ones on board the hospital ship were fine good nurses, but they didn't distract anyone. I think a nurse shouldn't be too pretty, or too ugly."

Nurses began to do the rounds of the rows of suffering patients in their beds in the large pleasantly-lit ward. The large table in the centre of the room had never been without bunches of flowers since the start of the war. Little by little, the men woke up. The clink of spoons in saucers and in porridge bowls, the smell of tea, coffee and, above all, of fried bacon seemed to have brought them out of their waking daze. And the men, who already had eggs and bacon in front of them, made the latecomers envious. Then those who could get up, got dressed in their indigo-coloured clothes, their red tie adding a subdued note to this atmosphere of whiteness and pallor.

When the "Doc" came to check the dressings, he found that all was fine for Dick and for Jim, who learnt that, as soon as his wounds were healed, he would be sent to Saint-Dunstan where the blind were prepared for their new life and where they would learn skills and occupations that would have them be more patient with their misfortune.

Jim was sad to think he would be separated from his mate. He also thought he wouldn't see Nurse Joan often. But Dick promised he would come and see him when he could and added that Nurse Joan would not forget her promise. They talked for a long time while smoking cigarettes and Dick listened carefully to Jim as he spoke about his life at *Lone Man Plain* and about the people he had left behind.

A little before lunch, Nurse Joan came to see them. She asked them straightaway how they had slept and how they were feeling. With a charity of spirit, but without seeming so, she chatted with Jim more than with Dick and, when she had her face turned from the blind man whose pulse she was taking by force of habit, Dick watched her and saw with pleasure that she lost nothing in the light of day. He noticed her hand on Jim's hand – a good hand to console and to do the dressings causing the minimum of pain. Something suddenly crossed his mind and, before he could think, Dick realised he had a small pang of jealousy like a slight, but sharp needle prick. It was only for a second, but the feeling of sadness was there, an ache that touches the heart when a woman you admire seems to take little notice of your presence. A hand placed on his hand chased away this momentary madness. Nurse Joan was feeling his pulse which began to race.

"It's a little fast," said Nurse Joan, "but not serious. I will come back when I can. Sometimes I have a sleep in the daytime when nights are overly busy and I am on duty. Bye now, both of you."

When she left, there was a silence. Jim and Dick didn't seem to have anything to say to each other for once. Perhaps they were trying to find a subject of conversation that had nothing to do with Nurse Joan.

There were a few Australians in the hospital. They had been put together and yarns were being passed on quickly from one bed to the next. Plans were made; they were already speaking about what they would see on their first outing: the Tower of London, Westminster Bridge, Madame Tussaud's, Piccadilly, Hyde Park and the Strand.

Will Bent, who owned a tobacco shop and barber's in Sydney, was naturally an expert on race horses. Many tips had been given in his shop and many bets had been made. He said he didn't give a damn about Westminster and the rest of the historical sites. George Street, Pitt Street and Sydney harbour was all he needed. He didn't expect to see anything better in London. But he would willingly go to the races in the country and put a pound bet on a horse.

"For us on the Lachlan," said Harry Lee whose head had been horribly split open and put together like terrine by military surgeons, "there's a spot called Bluegum Hole where there are seven homes, a store, a hotel and a police station. Once a year there are races at Bluegum Hole. Casey, the hotel owner, encourages horse racing and donates the prizes. Most of the horses and the jockeys belong to Casey; the races are generally won by Casey. After each race, we go to Casey's hotel to quench our thirst and, when the races are over, we are still thirsty. To cut a long story short, the district is in a hurry to give its hard-earned money to Casey and, at a time that varies between midnight and dawn, the district goes home to sleep thrilled with their day, leaving Casey equally thrilled with his day. Casey is making a fortune. One of these days he will be sent to Sydney to represent the district. No, he didn't join up; a man like him can't leave the district. It's us that have to have our coconut cracked, eh Charley! They can't say we didn't try!"

"*I* want to go to the London zoo to see the animals," said Charley Mitchell. "It's been a long time since I've seen any animals that aren't suffering, that don't have fear deep in their eyes. I remember a mule at Anzac Bay. Its mate had just been flattened by a bomb which had thrown the animal to earth, twisted like a half-empty bag. I saw its thin legs tremble while people were trying to release it from the mangled mass it was still attached to. Never have I been confronted with so much fear as in those eyes: they were deep like a well, a black well of fright. And the terror wasn't relieved even by a shout, or a whinny. All was emotionally contained and revealed only in the legs and the eyes. It was as if death circled a hundred times around the poor beast, touching it softly for its own amusement. It was horrible! The last time I saw Comet – that was her name – from a distance she looked like a unicorn for she had lost an ear. Deep in her eyes there was still fear, even when I caressed her."

In the far corner of the room, Skinner, sitting on his bed, propped himself up with one shattered shoulder that hadn't stopped him prying about in London as soon as his wound had allowed him to go out. Before leaving Australia, he had promised the editor of the *Taratoola Chronicle* that he would send him a few pieces about London. At Taratoola they were impatiently waiting on the column that 'our special correspondent' was going to write. Skinner had no pretention of being a journalist. In fact, at Taratoola he was the rabbit inspector which was no sinecure in a district where the cockies (farmers) had their grasses consumed by these pests. The government made him responsible for scouring the entire region, reporting on properties to see if the necessary methods to eradicate the plague were being used. Naturally, his honesty had made him a few enemies. Those owners who had had to pay a fine for not having killed their rabbits were angry with him. But, in general, Skinner was quite popular in the district. Moreover, he found this out when he left Taratoola station on his way to the "old country" as a volunteer.

Skinner carefully reread his notes on London for he knew the district was counting on him. He had not used long sentences as he was used to reports that were lacking in detail and a little dry which his excursions around the town of Taratoola suggested to him:

> *'Dead Cow Corner'*, Kerry's place, rabbits are everywhere; no sign of poisoning since the last rainfall, the fence wires are in poor condition. Kerry's property should be poisoned immediately, along with Kerry!

Up until now, his impressions of London were summarised thus:

Climate – London's climate has been decried a lot as the English climate. That's wrong. A month on the island has shown me that this unique climate has made the Anglo-Saxons who they are, the best colonisers in the whole world. My first impression with this climate was clear. I dreamt of how to get away from it.

Ever since there have been boats, the English, who have a little imagination and some intelligence, have gone on board after buying a ticket for anywhere provided there was some sun and money to be earned.

A world map will show you at first glance what their climate did for them; it has painted half of the globe in red.

London is too big.

In London there are some beautiful old churches, but many others throw out all accepted ideas of architecture and aesthetics. Some seem to have been built by children wanting to use blocks from their building boxes. Others look like garages or indoor skating rings. You go by without noticing them unless a large blackboard kindly advertises that the Reverend Smith will be preaching there next Sunday.

If you want to see London, go to Edgware Road of a Saturday evening. There you will see a huge crowd of people. Half of them are in the shops buying, the other half spend their time in the cinemas, theatres and in the pubs. One shop was hidden by crowded rows of customers. I managed to see above the people's heads that they were selling fish. Ornate notices were hanging from the ceiling. They bore the words: 'We have confidence in God'. I had to have someone explain what this meant by completing the sentence for me: 'But we ask men to pay in cash.' It would appear this advertising idea came from America.

The Australians disembarked in London at the wrong place, the military offices where they have to go when they arrive to receive their pay are in one of the most run-down areas of London. When a stranger is welcomed in a house, he should never be shown the backyard at first especially if it isn't nice to see! The poor wife with shawl and hat, the wino husband and their pale kids waiting at the pub door – this is the first thing an Australian sees when he arrives in London.

At Horseferry Road – the Australian Military Headquarters – two Australian soldiers arrived the other day, dirty, tanned and still wearing their putties. Their clothes were covered in the grey mud of France. They hadn't shaved for days and had the distinctive mark of men coming from the trenches. The cashier gave them what they were owed and then asked them, as he always did to those recently disembarking, if they wanted the address of a simple inexpensive hotel where they wouldn't risk being robbed as if they were in a lonely wood. One of the soldiers, the dirtiest, thanked him saying they had booked rooms at the Carlton. So they got in a taxi and were driven to the palatial Carlton Hotel.

A carriage passed close to me, a vision of all that is outmoded and from another era. The horses were certainly not ponies, but their harnesses were at least a hundred years old. The aging driver, wearing a pantomime livery, was driving a rococo barouche that bore a large coat of arms (like a label for a bottle of cognac) with a very old woman snoozing behind her veil. I am convinced that this upright guy doesn't know it is 1916, or that fighting is going on almost everywhere in the world.

There are too many women. I saw 40,000 in a procession one Saturday afternoon. That's much too many all at once!

English women have beautiful complexions. At times they over-emphasise it. They smoke a lot of cigarettes. Their maids take the children out while they walk their dogs.

Some of the female population seem to believe that the Australians came here to get married. Some Australians begin to believe that themselves. There are those who, distracted momentarily, were married in London forgetting they had already married legitimately in Australia.

There are too many stray dogs. I have suggested several efficient ways of destroying this pest. In London there's one, but I am told the idea is not practical and would create a revolution.

The Tube. – one of the most widely-used ways to travel in London. You can buy your ticket at first and, for the cost of three-pence, you can go from Charing Cross to Golders Green very quickly shaken a lot on the way.

The carriage interiors are interesting with a strange varied collection of humanity seen there. The first impression is terrible and can be roughly interpreted as: 'My God, how ugly we are!'

Fortunately, the ads on the ceiling are distracting. Between the name of a business that makes perfect attachable collars and a brand of a well-known and well-appreciated whisky, there is a verse from the Bible.

Life is becoming expensive in London. Advice in each compartment indicates the following tariff: 'Spitting is banned, fine of forty shillings'.

There is nothing attractive about the Strand. Tobacco and second-hand trunks are sold there. It is Sydney's George Street, but there are no awnings to shelter the footpath from the sun.

A night scene in the Strand. – at 11.30 in rain that hadn't stopped all day long, a man with his feet still in the stream of water was silently offering shoe laces to a few rare passers-by. But at this time of night no one seemed to need laces. A woman in rags arrived, carrying in her left hand a few boxes of matches that she protected under her shawl. She stopped in front of the man and asked abruptly: 'How much have you made today?' The man rubbed his white beard and said: 'Not enough to have much to eat.' The woman's eyes shone. 'A fine man has just given me half a crown,' she said trembling with emotion. 'And he didn't even take a box. Come, we're going to eat and drink something warm. I'm also really hungry!'

The man put the tangle of laces he was selling into his overcoat pocket and followed the woman into a laneway that lead to the Thames. She chatted brightly as if she were a little girl: 'We'll have a good warm coffee, sausages and mashed potatoes, bread and butter. See, there are still some fine moments in life even if pretty rare, aren't there?' The old man mumbled something very vaguely. They entered a low room, and the woman ordered for two. She gave her half crown to the waiter. It was the rule at Donato's always to pay in advance. They were content to be seated on a wooden seat with their elbows on the table. They were silent already imagining eating this meal that was so near with the smell of it filling the room. The boss suddenly appeared and said to the woman: 'Get out or I'll have the two of you arrested. Your money is counterfeit.' And he angrily thumped the half crown onto the table.

They didn't move for a few seconds then they understood and left in silence. Out in the street, the man said to the woman: 'Thank you anyway. It was beautiful for five minutes.' They were going to separate and disappear into the night – each in their direction when I called them. I had seen everything. I gave them each a half crown, a real one. I had never had so much of a life drama for five shillings.

London breeds a huge number of nutcases of both sexes. Near Victoria Station a man pushes, on a four-wheel carriage for infants, a cardboard boat on which are written religious maxims. In Knightsbridge, an old woman with a painted wig and wearing a very short dress walks an antediluvian dog on a leash dressed in a crocheted cardigan. Men in threadbare fitted coats, wearing top hats, gloves and shoes that shout poverty, pass by like sad ridiculous marionettes. Each Sunday the mentally deranged of London who are still not institutionalised gather together in Hyde Park to discuss religion, atheism, politics, suffragettism or even retirement pensions for old crippled cats.

You cannot bathe as you would like in the Thames. You have to know when it is low and high tide. Otherwise there's a risk you'll find yourself in a ridiculous position stuck in the mud that lines the wharves.

Skinner parcelled up his dispatch and addressed it to the *Taratoola Chronicle*. Then he lit a cigarette and anxiously wondered whether Taratoola would find its special correspondent up to the task. Jim had dozed off with his cigarette still in his mouth, fortunately not alight. Dick wasn't listening any longer to the yarns, but to the noises in the street which he couldn't see. He tried to comprehend the ceaseless rumbling of London. It was the continual sound of motor vehicles going by with banging and screeching of gear changes. It was the raucous siren of a tugboat floating under the bridge. There were loud noisy bumps on the wooden cobbles of a brewer's harness. And dominating all this, whistles that seemed to answer each other never stopping, even at night. Dick had to ask a nurse what those whistles meant as they obsessively filled the air. This was how he knew that the maids, servants and hotel porters of London hailed a taxi.

Jim still couldn't go out when Dick was given permission to go for a walk. He had to find another mate and he chose Bert who was also about to go on his first outing. They went along Victoria Street happy just like children strolling and looking at the shop windows that most caught their attention: tobacco and jewellery shops were certainly the ones that held them the longest. Their first purchase was a pipe. They each had a few pounds in their pockets and so they chose a good brand, a tobacco pouch and some matches. A policeman showed them the way to Hyde Park.

"I have never liked policemen," confessed Bert with a knowing air, "but I like the London police. They seem to take care of busses and children's carriages without wanting to be a nuisance to people. Yet they mustn't be easy-going when you've drunk a bit and they show you the way to the police station!"

In Hyde Park, they looked intensely and critically at a few horses and their riders who were trotting down Rotten Row. The animals were certainly not the ones London is proud of. They were the ones the army had not taken. They must have been rare as well, these carousel animals, for a woman on a bike was leading a pony with a little girl on its back having her riding lesson.

Dick and Bert then watched sheep wandering, crossing the pathways, seeking adventure and bleating occasionally. London's atmosphere wasn't great for the herd as the animals seemed, at first sight, to be moist haystacks. The two men listened to the bleating, visibly satisfied. Their nostrils were pleased to inhale the faint odour of suint like an old acquaintance. The sheep filed in front of them. Some were limping and must have had foot rot. Others had what Bert called the 'mark of the devil'. He thought their fleece wasn't covered entirely with wool. Besides, the herd had in their eyes the fault of being 'long wools', not merinos which, for the Australian, are the aristocrats of sheep.

When the two men reached Marble Bar, they were shown "Number Two bus" that would take them to a few yards from Madame Tussaud's. Dick and Bert spent a good hour and a half amidst kings, queens, noble men and the best known criminals. Royalty seen so close up; poisoners and assassins, considered calmly, disillusioned them. The grandeur of some and the terror of others had weakened.

"I'm pleased to have seen Napoleon's carriage and everything he owned," said Dick.

"I didn't know that they had had so many kings in England," said Bert. "Queen Elisabeth I mustn't have always been very pleasant. This has made me hungry, I could easily eat, what about you?"

In the afternoon, they visited Westminster Abbey. The day's program was probably not a particularly jolly one, but they wanted to see what they could of London. They were taken by the architecture as it was the first old church they had ever visited. There had been so much work and such care taken to decorate a roof and ceiling. The strange shape of the columns, doors and windows, the gates made of chiselled iron bent to resemble lace. They found all these things difficult to comprehend at first. They still hadn't accepted the need for art, this refined gourmandise for the eyes, a sensuality they had never come across before, at least that's what they thought. Dick forgot that when he made a stockwhip handle from myall wood, he would admire the shine he had patiently given the timber so that the marbled veins of fibres would stand out. When the handle was polished, he wasn't happy with its fine simplicity, he'd begin sculpting primitive shapes, diamonds, clover leaves, wavy lines and stars. Then he would place copper nails and inlay lead in it, always increasing the motifs. He was an artist in his way without knowing it.

Two years before, Bert had bought a silver watch. He had chosen a guilloche box engraved with garlands, in the middle of which his initials had been lovingly intertwined. This was his artistic taste and it was this taste that made him admire a saddle decorated with carved leathers, with learned complicated stitching. Or a bridle with each buckle a miniature horse made of nickel-plated iron.

But as for architecture, they didn't know the beauty of a diagonal-ribbed or trefoil arch. They had no comprehension of it. Despite this, they admired it and, slowly as the guide showed them the different tombs of kings and queens and those of important men, they felt as though they were impregnated by the atmosphere which Westminster Abbey is filled with. The sombre chapels, the dark corners shining with gold features, the stones they were walking on – all this was haunted by those who slept there for eternity. Dick and Bert were struck by sounds they heard from one end of the nave to the other. People walked with care speaking softly as if they were actually in the presence of this powerful noble gathering. The veneration for what has the grandeur of age and, at the same time, immortal glory was in each atom of this church and they felt it as if it were a thick penetrating fog.

When they left, they looked up and breathed with relief as they saw daylight which dazzled them momentarily.

"There's no doubt about it, it's beautiful," said Dick.

"Yes indeed!" was all Bert could add.

CHAPTER IX

Jim had arrived in Saint-Dunstan's Hospital a month earlier. It was a large building in the middle of a beautiful garden enclosed in Regent's Park, London. The matron welcomed him in the vestibule and had him follow the narrow carpet that went from one room to the next to help guide the blind. She had the voice of an older sister which immediately reassured him. He felt, from the very beginning, that everything she said was true. The guests at St-Dunstan's were happy. They could be heard whistling and singing. They worked with enthusiasm in their workshops, went rowing on the lake, often played music and once a week on Fridays they had an evening dance.

The matron introduced Jim to two other Australians who brought him up-to-date with the new world he was entering. They were the only 'colonials' and the only men in uniform. The other blind men were in civilian clothes and wore their regimental badges in their buttonholes.

The first fortnight had been difficult for Jim, but all the time he felt the presence of the women who were patiently looking after them. They took the patients to the park, chatted with them, read to them when they were not busy in the workshops, in the study rooms or the chook yards.

Jim decided to study Braille and raising poultry. He threw himself into his new occupations a little like a vigorous swimmer in cold water. There were about thirty students who were doing the theoretical and practical courses in raising poultry. They were taken first to the specimen fowl yard which had a collection of fifteen different types of chooks. They were given each fowl to hold and were instructed how to recognise each variety by the head, crest, plumage, legs and digits. The Livourne and the Ancona were the two types the blind could not distinguish from each other as they were differentiated only by the colour of their plumage.

The matron had given Jim a special watch for the blind. He could feel with his fingers the position of the hands from the raised spots placed before each hour. That morning, quite visibly impatient, he consulted his watch. He got up and walked a few steps into the large room with his walking cane in his hand. His hands had already acquired a hesitant and inquiring manner and his ear became more astute and ready to pick up sounds around him. In his pocket he had a letter from Nurse Joan. A Sister (not a Nun) had read it for him after the morning breakfast.

Dear Jim. I will come for you tomorrow at 11 o'clock and we'll go wherever you wish. We'll have lunch in a small restaurant I know in Jermyn Street. Sincerely – JOAN.

He had not yet lost his taste for tobacco. He stuffed his pipe and exhaled the smoke up to the ceiling, his dark glasses raised as if his poor eyes could still read everything written in the blue clouds of smoke from his pipe. There was only twenty minutes to wait and he thought with satisfaction that he would have Nurse Joan to himself for a whole day. Sometimes she went out with his mate Dick. He really liked Dick, but he couldn't hide a feeling of jealousy which wasn't strong, but was, nevertheless, quite real. Dick saw her and could speak to her with his eyes and see what her eyes were saying in return. One day, Dick told him that she resembled the Russian princess they had noticed in

Cairo at Shepheards' Hotel. Everyone admired her. Only, added Dick, the Russian seemed to have been kissed by the devil one day while Joan had never had anything to do with the devil. Speaking in this way, Dick must have admired her.

The day they spent together, they had not spoken of Nurse Joan. They had gone to Regent's Park. Jim had asked him to take his arm only when they were crossing a road for he already felt a little independent and proud not to accept attention that was overly attentive. He wanted to get rid of a constant helper. As they went by a house in Abbey Road, Jim said to Dick: "This is Abbey Lodge, a dwelling surrounded by a large garden. I would recognise it from all those in London. In a taxi or a bus. I know when I am going past this one for it smells like a skunk."

Dick pulled a face and said: "By Jove, you're right. It really does have a horrible strong smell."

Jim said: "Here we are at the lake. This is where we're going to train for the races. At St-Dunstan's there are boys who really know how to row."

Dick replied to his mate: "And here you get the better of me. With only one wing, I can't do such things any longer."

Jim recalled this encounter and had almost finished his pipe when Nurse Joan came into the room before he was aware of her presence. He was thinking of something else and hadn't paid attention to the sounds around him.

"How are things going?" asked Nurse Joan. "I think you've put on some weight."

"I'm quite well, thank you," the blind man answered obviously happy with one hand feeling somewhat feverishly for the buttons on his jacket.

She helped him put on his overcoat in the vestibule and they walked out arm-in-arm like lovers.

In the street, he often felt a wave of sadness when he heard girls laughing as they came alongside him and passed by. The laughs would stop suddenly; they would speak very softly, but not low enough for him not to hear their words: 'He's blind, poor man!' More than once, he wanted to tell them not to pity him, that their commiseration was a severely tight bandage containing boric acid that burnt his wound and did harm instead of healing.

"Do you want to go to the Zoo?" asked Nurse Joan. "It's about ten minutes from here."

"Yes," said Jim without hesitating, serene again. "I love animals."

Walking along the canal that edged Regent's Park, Joan looked around in the trees searching for something. Suddenly she took some peanuts out of her bag and gave them to Jim telling him to bend over gently so the squirrel would come and take the nuts from his hand. Jim squatted on his heels, with his hand held out and waited, patiently without moving. He soon perceived the sound of sharp nails on the bark of a tree. He heard the rustling of a few dead leaves and suddenly felt the nut taken from his fingers. And the squirrel, on his hindquarters with his tail in the shape of a question mark, began to open the nut, probably to see if it was good.

"It's a good one," explained Joan. "He's going to bury it and come back for another nut. There are still people who speak about animal instinct. It's something they have more than us, for they have intelligence and reasoning."

That set them off on the right foot.

"It's astonishing how ignorant we are about animals," Jim responded as they continued on their way. "We know that Australia is one of the oldest countries in the world, a country that was one of the first to be created then put to one side for centuries. The Dutch, the Spanish discovered it again, but didn't want it. It had to wait until Captain Cook discovered it for the fifth or sixth time to be noticed. We know that it has marsupials, egg-laying mammals, fish that cry and walk on land and oysters that grow on trees. But it is not six years since it was first discovered how a young kangaroo is born, how it manages to find its mother's pouch and grab on to her teat and no one is able to take it off.

People here have told me about snake bites. They explain quite correctly that they 'sting' with their forked tongue or their tail. It's this type of ignorance that is often the cause of the cruelty we saw in Egypt and which made us occasionally think that a paradise must exist for small donkeys. Ah! the poor little martyrs, so sweet and so patient, poorly fed, covered in wounds. If for them there is no fine paddock somewhere with beautiful long grass, a meadow where brutal man never comes to torment them, there's no justice in this world or in the next. All this suffering cannot be without some recompense!"

They came to the zoological garden. They went through the ticket office turn-style and turning left, crossed through the monkey enclosure which, despite the relative early hour of the morning, already had a good number of admirers. Jim couldn't help smiling when a small daring hand seized the nut he was holding through the fence netting. Nurse Joan explained its facial expressions.

"The grimace it has now, because he cannot get your peanut, is both a threat and a curse. For the same thing, man, the superior monkey, wouldn't show his teeth, he would use words, wish you hell and the most terrible things he can imagine."

They stopped in front of the sea lions' pool. Here could be heard from morning till night the large animals' hoarse barking. "Let's go and see the emu," said Jim who had just recognised a strange growling that seemed to come from a well. The birds stretched their necks above the bars and gobbled bread they were given. Jim felt a clumsy peck just pinch his finger.

"These birds," he said, "are a little crazy. You should see them flee in a paddock pursued by dogs. They run with the gait of a dancer in a short skirt, prancing, skidding, suddenly changing direction, its body one side, the neck and head the other. They are so grotesque it makes you fall from your saddle. They can be easily tamed when young, but they can quickly become impossible for they have to see and touch everything. They generally die because of this. We had one emu called

Micky who always troubled the horses as soon as he saw them tied up by their bridle. One horse, being a little ticklish and also finding Micky much too interested in its tail which he was pulling without consideration, lashed out at him with his hind legs sending the bird closer to the heavens than he had ever been. He landed back to earth a poor wreck of an emu."

He went on speaking. Joan guided him to a seat not far from there and was listening intently to him, careful to make sure he could sense she wasn't missing a word he said. For she knew that the blind love to speak about the past, things they will never see again. They love recalling everything that was in their past experiences, which is somehow the heritage that their sight left them before dying.

Several times, he stopped talking as if an idea got in the way. One hand went into the pocket inside his jacket and seemed to hesitate for a moment to reappear empty. Suddenly Jim lowered his voice and said to Nurse Joan: "I have a letter from home, it must be from my mother because father writes only rarely. This is the first letter I've received since becoming blind and I don't want to ask just anyone to read my letters from there. Nurse Joan, would it bother you to read it for me?"

"Of course not. I'll happily read it. Give it to me."

"It's taken three months to get to me," said Jim as a sort of preface as he handed it to her. She began:

Lone Man Plain 3 June 1915

My dear boy,

Where will you be when you receive this letter, if ever it gets to you? Your father and I are happy to know that one of ours is doing his part in the great work, but what we read in the newspapers engenders fear about all the dangers that lie in your path. We know that you will do what you have to do, and we pray that, if you are wounded, you will find all the goodness and kindness that are owing to the poor bleeding men of this terrible war.

We received your long letter from Egypt and the one from Gallipoli, but since then we know nothing of your doings. We remember that the postal services are disorganised and that the trunks are often late, this is indeed what helps us to patiently put up with the silence.

Nothing new here. These last months have been very dry, the lambing has given only 42 percent, flies have caused a lot of damage among the ewes. We are getting ready for the shearing but they say it won't be much, the animals have suffered and the wool will be short and easily broken. Your horse is fine. Father rides him from time to time to stop him becoming too fat. Your dog Darky hasn't forgotten you. He barks and whines every time someone says: Where's Jim?

Larkins is engaged to Rose Perkins. The small selector Green spent two years in prison for stealing sheep. He really deserved it. I have never liked that man. He always had a smile and a fist for everyone. Father is happy with this news. He is sure that it was Green who cut his fence wires in the Eagle Paddock. That's how Mrs Green got an expensive piano and sewing machine! They gave dances and 'at home' dos for this. Green is going to have 'at homes' for two years!

Fluffy has four little ones that are still furry all over. They are always near the barrel of molasses used for the phosphorous paste for the rabbits. These little dogs succeeded in covering themselves with molasses from the tap which always drips a little. Then they rolled around in the dirt and made a type of shell that made them look almost like tortoises. I had to melt the four of them in warm water, as if they were caramels. In the end, they left molasses and quite a lot of their fur at the bottom of my tub.

My boy, you will have seen some country overseas. The vast limitless sea, the pyramids of Egypt, and sand that is another ocean. Father told me the other day that you were fighting in Gallipoli not far from a plain where nations had fought for ten years over a woman. She must have been beautiful or men didn't have much to do in those times.

Perhaps you'll go to London. Let us know if you've seen the Thames, the King's palace, perhaps the king himself and the queen! Father doesn't say much. I know he misses you like I do. It's terribly sad to know that you are fighting there. It's wonderful as well, all sad things are generally beautiful. Why? We down here in the Antipodes are proud to send our men over there, to show the old world what they are worth.

A thousand warm wishes from both of us. Love you dearly.

God bless you, my boy.
YOUR MOTHER

Silence followed the reading. With his head lowered, Jim was still listening to the echo of those last words. Then he said: "Thank you, Nurse Joan."

"Jim," she said, "we are going to have to hatch up something together to answer your mother."

"We'll begin by sending her a cable which I'll ask you to write for me and send:

"Clarke, Lone Man Plain", Tallaponda,

New South Wales, Australia,

Good health, letter following

"JIM."

Joan reread the piece of paper with the dispatch written in pencil and promised to send it that day.

"I don't want them to know straight out that I have lost my sight. What can we do to have a letter sent to them without making them suspect something? I have often thought about this at night when I haven't been able to sleep. I've tried to write using a flat ruler on the paper, but Dick told me that all the letters with downstrokes were legless cripples cut off by the ruler's edge. They would guess immediately. The only idea I've been able to come up with is to tell them my eyes have been wounded and I have to wear bandages for a long time still."

Joan said: "I think that's for the best. You can dictate the letter and I'll write word for word what you say."

They stood up and went toward the bird cages. They were approaching a long flight enclosure when Jim stopped, glued to the spot.

"Listen," he said, listening hard. They could hear sounds as if they were notes made by a young child blowing a tin flute, repeating the same notes. "A maggie," shouted the blind man, "an Aussie magpie! Lead me to it. Have you something to give it?"

The magpie watched them draw near, turned its head on one side, its eyes alert and mocking. It jumped closer and took a piece of biscuit from Jim's fingers which Joan had bought as they entered the garden. Jim whistled, the bird let go of what was in its beak, listened with its head bent and began its trills and its flute ritornello.

Jim was enchanted. The magpie is the bird that starts waking people up at home first thing in the morning already thinking about tricks that bring happiness and despair to the family. Its song personifies Australia, embodying all that is there, smoke smelling of pine, fog at dawn that surrounds men lying around the embers of a dying fire and the gold dust of the sunsets which are like huge opals. Its song is in the air like the smell of gum trees. Australians love the magpie probably because it has their happy-go-lucky attitude and their mischievous behaviour.

South Australia has the magpie as its emblem. With its wings outspread and the tail fanned, Maggie makes its small heraldic effect.

"It's a bit of downunder," said Jim as they left the flight cage.

Nurse Joan found a taxi at the Zoo's exit. She helped Jim get into it and told the driver to drive them to the "Lauriers" in Jermyn Street.

Jim felt the gentle wind caress his face.

"We're crossing Regent's Park," said Joan. "We're going past Admiral Beatty's house ... now in front of Madame Tussaud's. Around Baker Street, there are houses with gates that still have, on either side of their doors, two large extinguishers which were used long ago to put out the torches. Now we are going in front of the Duke of Wellington's house. We're now in Piccadilly Circus with gentlemen's clubs all along; here's a women's club."

"What do the women do in their club?" asked Jim who was a little behind the times.

"They chat, smoke, have tea, invite men ... and many of them work hard."

"Do you smoke?" asked Jim in an anxious tone that made Joan smile.

"Sometimes," she confessed.

They got out at the "Lauriers" and sat at a small table. Joan read the menu for Jim and asked what he wanted. He chose lamb with vegetables.

"I would have thought you'd be tired of lamb," Joan said, "since you eat so much of it when you are at home from what you've told me."

"For us lamb is a little like bread. We don't easily tire of it. This war will really do Australians good. Those who return home will be worth two of those who never left. And one thing that struck us as soon as we disembarked in Egypt was the primitive method we use to cook in Australia. Someone said that we know a few different ways of spoiling our fine meat and the vegetables we have in abundance when we go to the trouble of growing them. In Cairo, we tried quite a few restaurants and we very quickly got used to continental cooking. In our country where summer is so hot, we need a simple, but enticing cuisine. A steaming leg of lamb on the table when it's 110 degrees Fahrenheit on the veranda is not always appetising. Especially when this *pièce de résistance* appears several times every week. We need a way of preparing it a little differently. We need variety in our cooking. People who camp don't have much time to cook complicated meals. They cut a whole sheep into slices, which they place in the frying pan as it is needed. Sometimes they even boil the meat in an old oil tin, but that's it. What's strange is that, despite our primitive taste, we are very difficult people. We mistrust dishes that we don't know and even vegetables we've never seen before."

Joan hesitated about where she could take Jim after lunch. She could only think of music to distract him and asked him if he would like to go to the Albert Hall where there was a concert. Jim loved music and readily accepted her offer. With her as his guide, he sensed he was entering a very large room. The echo of far-off voices gave the impression of distance, beneath a dome that could accommodate ten thousand people. He soon heard instruments being tuned. Joan read him the program.

She saw his hands move as the orchestra played Tchaikovsky's *Chanson sans paroles* and suddenly he squeezed her arm as hard as he could as if this music had entered him so deeply it caused him to suffer and the effort of squeezing was to stifle a loud cry that became lodged in his throat.

It was dark when Joan and Jim left the concert hall. They had to wait a long time for a taxi. Jim still had the music which had moved him so much in his ears. Gradually, the sounds softened and vanished like perfumed smoke dissipated by a breeze. It was as if he had somehow returned to earth. And the earth seemed to him, at that moment, to be terribly sombre and solitary. He suddenly drew closer to Joan and said in a hoarse voice: "Nurse Joan, you'll come back for me soon. I know that I'll feel very alone after today."

He took her arm in both his hands like a child and she let him, saying: "Yes, Jim, I'll come and get you next Friday. I can't come before then."

"In four days time then." he said, "Thank you so very much."

And when he got out of the taxi at St-Dunstan's, he repeated: "Thank you for today." He added softly: "You're not angry with me for taking your arm, it was a force stronger than me and I'm not yet used to…"

Nurse Joan reassured him and convinced him she wasn't angry about it. She then wished him a good evening.

CHAPTER X

Once he reached the porch, Jim knew his way straight along the narrow carpet. For the blind this was a sure path, but as soon as they left it, they became people using their hands to feel. They would hold them out in front to protect themselves from knocking into obstacles and seeking support.

In the large room downstairs, Jim could hear the organ. In one corner, a Sister was reading aloud. Further off two men were chatting. He recognised Murray's voice, the man who was in the bed next to his. Murray was the life of St-Dunstan's. The Director would like to have kept him as long as possible because of the happiness he generated. He came from Perth in Western Australia. He was barely five foot four inches tall and was given the nickname "Sawn-off". His face was covered in deep wrinkles of happiness and, despite the fact that his eyelids were always lowered, you couldn't help but notice humour spread across his face.

"Is that you Murray?" asked Jim going to the couch that went around the entire large room.

"Yes, old chap," replied the other man. "Come and sit down and tell us your news. You've been out with your girl. Where did she take you?"

The use of the word "girl" somehow shocked Jim, but he knew that Murray didn't intend to be unpleasant. However, he couldn't stop himself from correcting him.

"I went out with a nurse and we went to the zoo, then had lunch in town before spending the afternoon at a concert in the Albert Hall. I love music."

"I do too," said Murray. "I've never been able to sing in tune or whistle a true note. But I keep all the tunes in my head and, as soon as I hear the first notes, I easily come up with the piece. In Broome we had a Japanese diver in our team who taught me all I have in my head. He used to play the accordion like an artist, playing any tune we asked him to play including all of the world's national anthems. He was our best diver so he made quite a small fortune each season. And each season, the small fortune disappeared without leaving a bubble on the surface. He really liked sake and, when there wasn't any sake, he was satisfied with rum or gin. After having a few drinks, he showed remarkable energy in his work and the boss told him more than once that he stayed too long under water and that he went much too deep. One day, it was noticed he took too long to give the signal to be brought back up. Poor Ichiyamato! He was hauled into the boat inert. Once again, he had descended far too deep. He was dead. Now each time I hear an accordion, I think of poor Ichiyamato.

Joan came to St-Dunstan's after lunch as she had promised and wrote the letter which he had to send to his mother. She wrote as he dictated:

Dear Mother,

Thank you for your letter which followed me from Cairo, to Alexandria then to the Dardanelles to arrive finally here in London where I am on convalescent leave having been wounded in both eyes. It is not serious although it will be a long convalescence. You don't need to be worried about me. I have had to ask Nurse Joan to write this letter for me. I am really better than I have ever been and, if I tell you I now weigh 13 stone seven, you will understand I am not wasting away.

I am sorry to hear that the season has been bad for you. You should know you will have your strafing like others. You could believe the entire world is starting to expiate their sins and it doesn't look as if it is over. I have written a lot about my impressions of Egypt and I still remember them, clearly and profoundly – like hieroglyphics engraved in granite.

I haven't yet seen enough of London to have more than a vague idea about it. It's ugly, sad and bleak, but I feel, behind all this, is a whole universe of richness. There's nothing attractive at this time other than the parks, but a lot of things are imposing, giving you a sense of vertigo. I must say winter is not far off and fog hasn't changed my first impressions.

Everyone is very kind to me. I am taken by car or they hire buses for us and take us for walks everywhere. We go to the theatre, to concerts, we are invited for afternoon tea – all in all, Grandmother England really treats us like her grandchildren. It's good for the grandchildren in many respects. For some of them showed only a smidgen of respect and no reverence for our ancestors before leaving Australia.

The poor wounded are well cared for, you can be assured of that. There are thousands and thousands of women to look after and spoil them. They were on the hospital boat, kind and patient with us. They were here at the station to welcome us and take us to the hospital.

I am happy to know that Green is sheltered for two years. The poultry don't always get what they deserve. This one is well served. My wishes to all at *Lone Man Plain*, remember me to the boss and his family. Keep the best of Fluffy's pups for me. She is a thoroughbred and should produce good sheep dogs.

A thousand wishes for you and father, I love you both
Your JIM
My address till a new order comes will be:

Australian Military Headquarters

Horseferry Road, London (Westminster).

Joan left to post the letter and came back that evening to help with the dance. About 8.30 she approached him. He stood up and, holding the ramp that ran along the wall, showed her the women's cloakroom.

The large room had been emptied, the chairs and sofa had been placed against the walls and forty couples were dancing comfortably there to the sound of the piano, a violin and a cornet. Two things struck Joan as she entered the room: the sombre lighting in the ballroom and the gaiety of the dancers. The men who were not dancing were chatting with the young women who had come to distract them. Coquettishness was not dead amongst the blind for nearly all of them wore polished shoes.

The couples whirled around without bumping into one another anymore than in any ordinary ballroom. The dancers accompanied the orchestra by whistling or singing when the waltz was one they liked. Shouts of joy and "encores" acknowledged the final sequence of each dance and the Scottish Reel always ended amid wild shouts coming from the Scots who were there. Jim was happy to find Joan not wearing her nurse uniform. He wanted to know the colour of her tailor-made outfit. And approved of the plum tone. He felt proud dancing with her.

The matron walked around the room, being saluted by the blind men who recognised her voice. She was like a mother, a sister and a mate for them all. Their faces lit up when she went by which was touching to see. Everyone wanted to speak to her and she managed not to miss anyone. Jim introduced Nurse Joan. The two women exchanged a few words before Matron slipped away to dance with a blind man who seemed to have been forgotten sitting in the corner of the room. Despite her fatigue from her day's work, she went a few rounds of a waltz with the abandoned man and dutifully found him a partner.

"Do you want to dance with someone else?" Jim asked.

And Joan noticed his anxious expression which he had not been able to hide. "No," she said. "I want to stay with you."

Jim sank back onto a sofa while Nurse Joan lit a cigarette for him.

"Until now, us other tommies didn't know that such an angel existed here on earth. I think a lot of us would like to have an illuminating lightning flash lasting a second so we could see Matron's face. We do know it. It has to be beautiful for she is so good, so genuinely good, so bright. Take a long close look at her and tell me what you see, so that I can imagine her better in my mind."

Joan observed Matron who was now sitting near the small soldier called Brown. He had been at Loos, at Hooge and had been wounded thirteen times and had come back blind, having lost his right hand and three fingers on his left hand at the same time. He was busy thumping Matron on the back with his injured right arm just like a child would amuse himself with his mother or a maid. The noble woman was defending herself laughing and gently scolding her assailant for his dark ingratitude. Suddenly, Brown stopped hitting her and his poor mutilated hand squeezed Matron's hand to show her how much he loved her.

"Yes," said Joan, "she is beautiful – all that goodness, patience and sweetness show in her features. This woman would never be able to live away from those who need her help and her consolation. She lives only for her dedication. You are right to love her, all of you."

"Nurse Joan, will you take me to the garden? It's starting to get hot in the room. Do you mind?"

They crossed the floor as soon as the dancers had applauded the fox trot which was always the most successful.

"Are there a lot of stars out this evening?" Jim asked.

"Yes," she said. "They're all out."

"We have so many in Australia," said Jim sadly. "It could be said that the sower had upturned handfuls of them as he emptied the bag from his apron. I remember when our Southern Cross disappeared from the sky for the first time as we travelled north. It was for us the last link with Australia. From that moment on, we felt much further from the Antipodes and understood we were on the other side of the globe."

After a short silence, he suddenly asked: "Have you seen Dick recently?"

"No," Joan replied. "I haven't seen him for two weeks. We did go to the cinema one afternoon."

"Dick's lucky, he can see you. He described you for me one day. I asked him to."

"Well," laughed Joan, "did his description satisfy you?"

"He described you pretty much as you described Matron for me, only I know your eyes are dark brown, you have a lot of hair which is like burnt copper. That's what he said."

"It's true, my hair is red, but you can't see it when I'm wearing my white headgear."

"Can I touch your hair, Nurse Joan?"

She bent her head towards the blind man and he ran a hand through the thick tresses that formed a chignon low on the nape of her neck. She felt him remove one of the pins, but pretended she hadn't noticed.

It was late. They returned to the ballroom as the orchestra was playing "God Save the King". The blind men, the nurses and the invitees were all standing singing the National Anthem. The men's voices filled the large room as they thundered out this patriotic song, as they would have done in a church. They all asked that their king would be safe – this king who they had lost their eyes for; this king who they, while still young, had entered a night of deep horror and solitude for.

And Nurse Joan, who had seen much suffering and enough sadness to fill the memory and imagination of an entire lifetime, felt a tear flow as the last chords of the anthem were dying.

CHAPTER XI

One morning, Nurse Joan took the names of those convalescents in the hospital who wanted to travel to the country where they were invited to spend the day. There were twenty invitations sent to several hospitals in London. At first, Dick had hesitated to put his name to the list for he was thinking of seeing Jim at St-Dunstan's, but the sky was so beautiful and the sunshine so tempting he got ready instead to be taken to Charing Cross where seats had been booked for them on a train. They left at ten o'clock in the morning. Wearing indigo uniforms and red ties, the men were like children on holiday, smoking cigarettes as if each intake of tobacco was as necessary and as indispensable as air itself. Pleasant jibes were exchanged.

"Hello Stumpy!" shouted a one-arm man to his one-leg mate.

"Hello Wingy!" the man on crutches replied.

Crude adjectives flew around in the compartments – original, humorous and without malice. As the train started, a few kisses were blown to women who were not expecting them. But they replied with a smile and a wave of the hand.

The Anzacs were seated together. They got on quite well with the English and the Scots, but were happy to discover different countries and listen to what others had to say while they silently smoked.

Jock, who had only one leg, thought he would no longer wear the black-and-green kilt uniform or the red-and-white stockings that used to suit him so well. He thought with a profound sadness that a wooden leg wouldn't look good with the short skirt and he missed the leg he had left behind near Ypres. He had always been proud of his legs.

"Poor skittle," he said as he same out of the operation. "It was my closest relative and for sure the one I loved the most. We lived together without the mildest dispute for twenty-three years. It dragged me, I confess, where I shouldn't have gone, but did so to please me. It knew how to dance to the tune of the bagpipes and knew how to move like a crazy thing around the floor. When we played football, it showed those in the north of England what Caledonians could do in the field."

He then thought of Maggie who, without exactly being his fiancée, was extremely dear to him. Would she now say "no" because he had only one leg? At first, he was going to have one of those artificial legs they made at Roehempton. A solid light leg. That would allow him to walk and jump as before. And he promised himself he would write to Maggie that very evening for she hadn't answered the letter he had sent last week.

In a corner of the compartment was another amputee, the famous 'Biscuits'. He had retained the nickname. He was so used to it that he didn't think about it any more. He had been wounded rather seriously once in the knee when a crate of Huntley Palmers he was unloading fell on his knee sending him to the hospital. Jones had suffered as much as if he had been injured by shrapnel, but there was no glory in it. He set about to change this situation and to put some glory into his injury during his convalescence in London. He showed the splinters that had been removed from his knee and distributed a few to those around him. This gained him a measure of respect. He also deliberately limped.

Unfortunately for him, he went too far in this role-play. The biscuit story was circulated again in London and he left the capital in a cloud that had begun to cast a shadow on his reputation.

He was almost happy to return to the trenches where he was christened 'Biscuits' for the rest of his life. A short time later, a grenade hit his leg and he regained consciousness one morning in a hospital bed with one leg missing. And the nurses were so astonished to see him take the news of his amputated leg so serenely – he seemed almost pleased.

MacGaw, the Scot, was another in the group on the train. After a month of not being able to speak caused by a bomb explosion, he had found his voice a week ago when a tobacco seller had given him sixpence short of what he was owed. His mate Jock was with him at the time and said that the effect was dramatic. The very idea that someone could steal sixpence from MacGaw was in itself monstrous. But the language that suddenly was unleashed from Davy MacGaw's lips annihilated the tobacco salesman. Jock said it was like a barrage of fire and the sixpence was suddenly on the counter as if it had been newly minted.

MacRae of the AIF was sitting next to a nurse who frequently lit a cigarette for him and placed it in his mouth. MacRae seemed to be sitting nonchalantly in his corner with his hands in his pockets; in fact, he had no hands. He lost both at the same time on the Gallipoli Peninsula. "Wait till the artificial ones get to the United States," he said to the others. "I paid thirty dollars for them. The best thing is I'll be able to thread a needle, hold a pen or play cards as well as the rest of you. Provided they are not torpedoed at sea by the rotten Boches! Long ago, my mother used to say that she had never seen a kid who could dirty his hands so often and as easily as I did."

The Australians looked out at the passing countryside, at the tiny paddocks. Almost all the ewes had twin lambs.

"How's that for lambing!" someone said, "Two hundred percent."

Another man said, "The sheep are fed turnips every day. It must cost a fortune."

From the train, they first saw fields of packed roofs, these truncated forests of chimney pots, cottages grey from smoke and occasionally the gloomy interiors of the poor folk. Then there were the new towns made by the dozen like brioches. Suburbs were dotted along the way like an endless stream of a large flock. Next, they saw isolated houses, parks and residences that looked like small strong chateaux, so as not to go against the English saying 'An Englishman's home is his castle'.

All this countryside seemed to be a miniature of meadows surrounded by live hedges, a few acres, a few dozen sheep. Everywhere streams, fences, small clean cute cottages. Asphalt roads followed the track or went off towards the horizon. They had been told that there were roads everywhere and you could drive on the London asphalt right to Scotland.

Occasionally, they saw a man working with a single-blade plough and the Australians were always amazed at this treatment of the soil that appeared to them to be a system of stone-age agriculture. There was a young girl guarding four cows while she knitted. It was as if the cows were free to wander far in this piecemeal patchwork country.

Dick felt he would suffocate if he lived in this country: the small fields, woods where you could count the number of trees were private properties which you were not permitted to enter. If you wanted to make some tea, you would probably have to light a fire on the side of the asphalt road!

They all noticed that the ground was not very fertile. Old trees were seen, but there were no enormous, century-old ones. The ploughs brought up stones among masses of earth. The railway-line trenches showed sections of earth where the humus was only six or seven inches deep.

The idea of living in such a country where you could call out to one another from one tiny farm to the next did not tempt them. Every morning fifteen roosters, from fifteen different poultry sheds heralded the dawn. If you walked a few hundred yards, you came to what seemed to be a wall – the neighbour's hedge. It was oppressive! A hedge, a house or even a factory completely masked the horizon. These men loved their naked and distant Australian horizon; not like a loud wall-paper that tires the eyes!

"Give me back my two hands and give me a lot of money," said MacRae. "I don't think you would make me plant cabbages or turnips in this country. At first I thought a long winter spent here would soften me. I bet that if people knew how it's so easy to live in our country without becoming very rich, they would all hop on the first boat!"

A Canadian entered the conversation: "Canada is closer than Australia. We have long winters, but are they harder to endure than your endless summers? Fortunately, there's something for all tastes. I'm satisfied with rye country and, once the war has ended, I'm going back to see my Rockies and, later, if I have the money I'll willingly go and see your tiny island."

"While you are there," said the Waitaki Maori, "give New Zealand the once over. It's there you will find plenty of choice, plantations of banana palms, cold lakes, warm lakes, geysers, glaciers, virgin forests, tree ferns, fiords and even earthquakes and volcanoes. People who have travelled the world say they haven't seen anything more beautiful than my country."

"My country," said a one-eyed man, "is probably the ugliest, most disagreeable country in the world. There's only one tree which is small and grew in the governor's garden. The wind always blows there, all year long, rain and fog are more frequent than sunshine. We live there far from everything and, despite this, when the war is over, it will be the Falklands I buy my ticket to."

When they got off the train, a large carriage with several seats was waiting for them at the station. The small town had shops like the ones in the fine districts of London. The fruit shop displayed bananas and enormous grapes grown under cover. Like the fruit, huge bunches of flowers were waiting for a rich and prodigious clientele. Even the butcher's display had the appearance of a first-rate shop and the man with the blue-and-white striped apron, wearing his melon hat at an angle, came up closer than those in Piccadilly, closer even than the one in Edgeware Road. They felt they were in the cosy atmosphere of the gentry where only the expensive and the best was sold.

As they travelled on, cottages came after the shops, each with a small front garden and each bearing a name that varied from 'Mon Repos' to 'Bellavista', to 'Beauséjour' or 'Fairhome'. Every now and then, they noticed a drawing representing a Military Cross on the windows. There was one cottage with four crosses, one being adorned with black crepe. Each medal indicated a man of the house who had left for the Front.

Then the countryside began in earnest, marked by a hedge behind which were meadows, fields and small woods. A large open gate revealed pathways lined with trees that led up to a dwelling covered in ivy and virgin vines. There were many of these properties along the road, some grander and some less so, but all of them were well cared for so that they looked like public parks.

When the horses slowed down, the men looked at these neat pathways laid out like linoleum, lawns which they felt were springy and mown, like good quality woollen carpet. Some driveways were even made of asphalt and they could be walked on all the time in dance shoes. In the meadows, the cattle trimmed the branches they could reach with perfect regularity. These parks seemed to have been land-scaped as seen in an engraving, so that the entire picture was prefect in its regularity without being monotonous.

The Australians, who were most interested in this countryside, were happy to find a little of the peacefulness of their bush, but it seemed to them that it was more a drowsiness that could not last because the noise of a car coming along the road frequently disturbed it. It was, however, a tranquillity they willingly accepted after the continuous drive to get there and the incessant buzzing of London.

Birds singing in the trees, a song they did not recognise, long phrases that were certainly a conversation. Two young girls came beside them along the hedges bending down all the time to add to a scraggy bouquet they were carrying. They noticed their pink cheeks like small apples and their eyes pale blue like an Australian sky. They were dressed in strong bright colours. They remembered having already seen these children, a few years before, on Christmas cards. They had seen the hedges, the avenues and this idealised countryside in printed form.

The seated carriage went between the pillars of a monumental gate and entered into a pathway lined with huge rhododendrons. A curve made it disappear about 100 metres ahead. The manor appeared suddenly, lording it over a large lawn terrace and its roofs, with chimneys and numerous narrow windows, looking at the outside world behind their lead lighting, made the building look like something from another age. An elderly man was waiting on the porch for the guests. He helped the two nurses down from the carriage while the servants took the crutches and supported those convalescents who were still not sure of their balance as they left the footing. The host shook each person's hand as they entered the large vestibule and for each he had a kind solicitous smile.

When the men had removed their overcoats and their caps, they were escorted into the living room and were at first taken aback by everything they saw in the huge room. They looked at the paintings and the fine old tapestries on the walls and forgot to sit down.

The host thought charitably not to make them wait for lunch and the guys showed their upright behaviour by pretending to be indifferent when they heard the announcement that the meal was served. The table was a vision of whiteness, flowers and silverware. The old man indicated to a nurse the place facing him and asked the other nurse to sit on his left. He put the men at ease asking them to sit wherever they liked. The servants, circulating around the table, carried out what the men saw as a kind of banquet. They were grateful that this perfectly stylised and somewhat imposing group of employees did not present each dish ceremoniously, but served them with a preconceived idea that their appetite would not be offended by large portions.

The host took turns in speaking to some of the men and then others, recounting stories of his youth and quickly chased any discomfort that could often exist at the start of a meal where many guests were gathered together.

"Sam," said Lou quietly to his neighbour, "it's the first time in my life that I have sat at such a fine table. Look, four forks, four knives and not all the same! It reminds me of our three pronged fork with a bone handle and our knife that was cleaned each time by sticking them into the ground. Look at the silver salt shakers and the bottles of pickles! They're beautiful, but it's all complicated. And the knives are sharp. You have to be extremely careful if you are served peas!"

All were honoured at the lunch. MacRae was next to one of the nurses and she and the person next to him helped him eat. The 'adoptive parents' had work to do, for MacRae had a remarkable appetite compared with the solid appetites of others at the table. Fortunately for Lou's good reputation, there were no peas on the menu that culminated with the complete demolition of bowls of beautiful fruit. They then went into the huge billiard room where coffee was served, while the host offered cigarettes and large expensive cigars with a gold and vermillion band around them.

The guests willingly accepted the invitation to see the garden. The autumn sun gave all the warmth and splendour it had, highlighting the bright green of the lawns and the intense red of the virgin vines that partially covered the walls of the building. Like many constructions started in the reign of Queen Elizabeth I, this building took the form of a capital E. Its diverse pointed roofs and numerous mullioned windows maintained perfectly the building's original character. The convalescents noticed a sun dial dated 1639 in front to the terrace. Dick and his Australian mates examined it with curiosity.

"In a country where there is so little sun," said Dick, "these instruments don't wear out quickly! It's more than two hundred and seventy years old, Bill. At that time, Australia was patiently waiting to be noticed, standing on the sidelines, eh? It makes you giddy to look so far back in time."

Three quarters of an hour later, they all returned to the hall and groups formed around a large display of daggers of the most diverse shapes, swords and double-edged claymores. These men, who had just suffered a modern war, were curious and interested to see close up these instruments of suffering. The host showed them how to handle an Italian misericord which, by pressing a hidden spring, would spread into three sections and become a sort of trident with each blade capable of inflicting a different death.

"This molten morion," said the host, "and the sword opposite are part of the history of this property and this house.[3] Families have succeeded each other here for several centuries and generations. One wing of the dwelling was burnt and rebuilt twice, but this hall, the dining room and the kitchen are as they were when they were first built. About three hundred years ago, the man who lived here wanted his son to marry a rich woman in the neighbourhood. But the son's will was hard to manipulate, either that or his heart was not free to give to another. The father tried everything, even threats, but nothing succeeded. One day when both of them were armed from head to foot in readiness to leave for war, the knight asked his son once more to marry the woman he had chosen for him. The son drew his sword from its sheath and said ..."

At this moment, a voice was heard coming from among the attentive convalescents and, before the host had time to draw breath, it took up the storyline...

"By this brilliant blade like a ray of sunshine, by all the fibres of this pure steel blue as the moon, I swear I will never ever marry anyone except the woman I choose. Then the knight, in a movement of rage,

---

3   A morion is a soldier's helmet used in the 16th and 17th centuries.

brandished his sword. The son saw the weapon lift over him, he didn't move his arm, he didn't make the least movement to ward off the blow that opened his helmet like a piece of ripe fruit and struck him down dead at his father's feet."

The story had been interrupted for only a few seconds. The voice was younger, yet stronger and with its intonation resembled an old man's voice.

The elderly man had turned his head like his listeners had done to Dick's voice. The host had turned pale and the nurse closest to him helped him sit in an armchair while she indicated to the guests to leave the room.

Dick didn't move. He stayed there alone, with his eyes fixed on the molten helmet. At first he didn't hear the old man's words.

"Your voice is a ghost's voice … and this story, you finished it word for word with *his* voice. How do you know it?"

"My father often told it to me and I often repeated it."

"What's your name?" the elderly host suddenly asked.

"Richard Jerry … my father was called Bernard."

"Your name is actually Jeromey, mine … you are my grandson …"

"I thought so as soon as I saw the display."

He realised that the old man wanted to ask him a question. He hesitated, his lips trembled, only his eyes dared to ask and Dick understood. "My father died about six years ago now."

"Richard-Bernard Jeromey, I am an old man. I stayed back here while all the others left – my wife, my daughter and my son. I was kept so that I gathered together all the sadness that the others left along the way. I am the straggler, my feet knocked the stones that the others dislodged from the path. Sit down," said the old man as he firmly grabbed Dick's hand. "Did your father talk about my anger? One day I wanted to impose my will on him and he refused … and left for I have never known where. He never wrote to me, or gave me any indication of where he was."

"My father said nothing against you, not one word. I guessed there had been something very sad and, since my mother died some fourteen years ago, he often spoke to me of his childhood, but never a single word of bitterness or complaint."

"I am very proud of you, Bernard. You have come from down there to fight. He would have done the same, I know. Bernard, you are my grandson, the only one who is left. All I have is yours."

But Dick, in silence, was thinking. "Did my father do something so serious that he had to go halfway round the world to hide what he had done?"

"No," said the old man. "There was a terrible misunderstanding. We were both good mates, like father and son should always be. But we both have an iron will and we didn't want to give in, neither of us. A gesture from me sent him into exile. Since he left, I have done everything to find him to bring him back and, if I hadn't been so old, I would have left myself in search of him. Now after these long, lonely years, I have found you … Will you live with me? I know that for you as for me it is something so sudden we cannot yet believe that this meeting is real, nor realise the change it could bring in our lives. I leave you to think on it, the time to return to this dream which is stranger than many. Give me your answer soon."

There were repeated hurrahs when the old man went out onto the terrace and announced to his guests that the man they called Dick was his grandson. Dick felt the beginnings of an inner conflict. He could see, in front of him, his father – sombre and silent for long moments. He saw his grandfather now. He had found the person who had caused the silence and had amassed the sadness around his father. The old man wanted him to stay near him. He would have to renounce returning to Australia. He would be a rich man envied by his mates, him the rabbit and possum trapper!

What would his father do in his place? What would he have advised? Leave the old man to go back to his solitude? Forget an outburst of anger that had been a blow his father had probably died from years after!

And Dick murmured between his teeth: "The son saw the weapon rise over him, he didn't move ..."

It was time to leave. The old man wished all his guests a good trip and then he said to Dick, squeezing his shoulders: "I'll wait for your answer. I understand your hesitation. An hour cannot wipe out twenty years. But I'll be seeing you again soon. Do you need any money? Ask whatever you wish?"

Dick replied that he had everything he needed and his remaining hand touched his pocket that contained one shilling and eight pence, a knife and a pipe.

"God bless you," said the old man as he shook his hand.

And Dick felt a need to throw himself around the old man's neck. But there was some force inside him that held him back – will and pride – the same will and pride that had already damaged two lives.

CHAPTER XII

"Have you ever taken tickets in the Tattersall lotteries?" asked Sewell, a native from Camoorajingalong, a place in New South Wales which had thirty-seven inhabitants. "I've been regularly putting a pound sterling on a horse in the Melbourne Cup for nearly ten years. Up until now, it's Tattersall and Co who have won. Dick isn't at all a gambler. I've never even seen him play cards. Today a huge lottery has fallen his way, a property worth thousands and hundreds of pounds and he doesn't even react. He stays calm. You could almost say he is wondering if it's worth the trouble to bend and pick it up."

"Just his grandfather's house," added Nash, "the paintings and their frames, the silver and the furniture, that would be enough for me!"

"If something like this happened to me," continued Sewell, "first, I would give a party for my mates they would never forget and then I would breed race horses."

"That's where we differ," said Dick. "I don't care for your race horses. I don't like the atmosphere of the racing stables and I wouldn't go two yards to see a race. First, all your races from the biggest to the smallest, are con jobs, arranged, bought or stolen in advance. Races have their good side in spite of everything. They get money from those who don't know what to do with it and circulate it. No! Sewell, find me something other than your horse races."

"If you don't like that," said Nash, "there's cars. Buy yourself a Rolls Royce 80 horsepower and travel. Go to the continent, to Paris, Nice, Italy. Travel is still the best way to spend money. It always stays with you and the memory of it stays with you until you die. If you need a good chauffeur, Dick, even an honest one, I warmly recommend myself. I have driven cars in the bush. Not in London or Paris, that would frighten me after *Plum Pudding Creeks*, the *Glue Pots*, the sand hills or the black earth plains I had to cross in New South!"

"That's all very tempting", said Dick, "but, in my case, I have to think about it and need to readjust my mind before seeing exactly how it sits with me."

On the train before arriving in London, discussions continued about the quickest way of making a fortune melt like a piece of butter in a frying pan. All of the ways suggested were good, from mining or horse speculations to land investments, raising angora rabbits, ostriches or pearl oysters.

Dick was still looking for a solution to this problem that had just disconcertingly and suddenly fallen from above into his lap. He remembered the old man's confession of loneliness, his prayer that he didn't want to be abandoned, left alone on this earth. He had paid heavily for one angry act and for years he had tried to find the son he had driven away.

And during those long years, Dick's father had waited, not wanting to call. He would have wanted to return home to England, but he refused to take the first step. This had been a struggle between two proud wills, two stubborn people – father and son.

It was too much for Dick's poor brain to cope with. He fell asleep late that evening with his mind and heart drawn every which way. Suddenly, he thought of Nurse Joan. He would see her and asked her advice. He was sure she would be able to help him come to the right decision.

Joan replied to his written request making an appointment to see him a couple of days later. She took him to lunch in a small grill in Knightsbridge. He told her what she didn't know about his father and the strange chance meeting he had with his grandfather.

"This war," claimed Joan, "brings families closer who have been forgotten or lost for fifty years. Australians and New Zealanders have unearthed relatives everywhere in the UK, even in the far north of Scotland. But I confess your meeting is not ordinary. I can understand you cannot forget your father's many years of sadness. It's natural that, in your child's imagination, the image of your grandfather has taken on characteristics that are in no way cheery. Your father was a just and fair man – that's how I think of him. If his voice could come to you from the beyond, what do you think it would advise you to do?"

"I believe it would tell me to stay with my grandfather," Dick replied.

"That's also my conviction; it's your duty worked out. A duty which isn't that difficult to carry out. Come on Dick, you have it in your power to make the few years that remain for an old man to be happy ones. An old man who is your father's father. It's a beautiful thing to be able to give happiness!"

Joan felt a very quiet satisfaction in knowing Dick had decided to carry out his duty.

"You know," she went on after a long silence, "that Jim isn't well. Winter is hard for him. I would like him to be able to go back to Australia for health reasons. Would you be able to help me make him decide to do this? He knows the climate here doesn't suit him and he knows that he can return to his family. He doesn't want to hear any one speak about him leaving. He doesn't give any reason. He just simply says 'No'."

Dick looked Nurse Joan squarely in the face and in such a strange way that she took a slight step backwards. "It would be too difficult for him to leave you." said Dick. "An idea he has in his head!" And Dick thought that the blind were not the only people deprived of sight.

After leaving Dick, Joan went to St-Dunstan's where the matron welcomed her and immediately spoke to her about Jim. He was coughing a lot, was very depressed and seemed to be withdrawn, as if the outside world no longer interested him. For a few days, he had not wanted to get out of his emotional paralysis and the matron – who was not aware of some of the reasons that caused the blind to suffer – did not know how to distract him from his dark thoughts. She asked Joan to be kind enough to wait until he came out from his Braille class and try to boost his morale. Joan went and sat in a room where a few blind people were busy making threads on a circular frame held between their knees.

She had heard Australians coughing all over London. They seemed frozen in their large overcoats and their large brimmed hats appeared, like their wearers, to be out of place in this atmosphere of rain and yellow fog. She has seen them around the fire at the Anzacs buffet, forming a tight circle and talking about the country down there where there was sunshine – often more than was wanted...

They had lost the tan that made them stand out at first. And their broad shoulders stooped from long horse rides seemed to bend further under the cold, lead-like grey atmosphere of London. They spoke about consumption and pneumonia and Joan was fearful for Jim. His cough frightened her.

He came in, walking straight on the carpet strip, at a slow pace but without hesitating. He was beginning to feel more sure of himself. Joan went to meet him, wishing him good afternoon. She found that he had become thinner and, with each bout of coughing, his large body shook ever so pitifully.

"Jim," she said anxious to get to the point, "you have to ask to leave here by the first available transport ship going to Australia. This climate doesn't owe you anything. We are approaching winter and there are still four months of cold ahead. Your lungs are at risk. And a change of temperature will bring you back to health quickly. You will be cured before you get to Port Said."

With his head lowered, Jim seemed to have nothing to say to this.

"And your parents? Don't you want to see them again? You could look after yourself with them and they will have you with them and you will again be with your beloved *Lone Man Plain*."

"Yes," said Jim bitterly, "the Plain of the Lonely Man! That's the place for me! Nurse you have all sorts of good reasons to have me leave England. Why do you want me to go? Everyone coughs in this country!"

Joan placed a hand on his arm: "I want to know you are out of this climate, because I'm interested in you, because I am convinced that it's for your good. I only ask you to be reasonable."

She felt Jim's silence would not give her much hope. She guessed how fixed and stubborn his mind was. She suddenly changed the subject. "Do you know what has happened to Dick? He has found his grandfather in the countryside of Tunbridge Wells and I think that he is now the wealthy inheritor of a huge fortune."

"Dick has all the luck. He has one arm and has become rich. He can marry as he wishes. I don't like Dick the less for that. I'm happy about his good fortune and I hope to see him before too long."

"And the poultry raising, how's that going?"

"Yes," said Jim, "we have another exam in three days so I have quite a bit of work to do."

"I can only just distinguish a Plymouth Rock from an Aylesbury. I fear that, if your examiner saw the name Joan, he would give a very bad mark! I do so like the country and I have never had time to see any other trees except those in Hyde Park. I sometimes dream of a week's leave when I would take time in the country without doing anything with my ten fingers or my brain. I think that if we are allowed to live, from time to time, like vegetables with as many thoughts and cares as a Milan cabbage or a lettuce, it would do us an enormous amount of good. Our machines, horses, dogs rest completely while they sleep, they abandon their work in nothingness. We can never do that. And we wear ourselves out quickly! ... Jim, if the weather is reasonable, I'll come and get you next Saturday afternoon and we'll go to a concert."

"With pleasure, thank you," the blind man replied.

She left him feeling that if she hadn't been able to make him decide to leave, she had turned his mind from his dark thoughts at least for a little while. Nevertheless, she remained very worried to see him like this. She scarcely dared admit the fear she had that he would relapse – this poor man who walked on the edge of a precipice always feeling his way. A false step was so easy and it would not take much for his despair to push him off with the slightest tip of its wing!

Joan did not go to St-Dunstan's as she had intended. Nurse White came in her place and gave Jim a letter which she read to him.

Dear Jim

There's a boat leaving in three weeks for Australia. I have just been offered a place on board as a nurse and as I know how a change will do me good, I have decided to accept the job. If you want to apply for a passage on this transport ship, it would give me pleasure helping you and apply pressure wherever possible with the necessary formalities. Nurse White will write your answer, if you want to dictate it to her.

Sincerely

JOAN

Jim asked Nurse White to give him a few minutes to think about it. But without him being aware of it, the decision had already been made. It had come as soon as he had heard the first lines of the letter. No, he wouldn't be able to stay here knowing she had gone down yonder. At least that's what he believed.

He asked Nurse White to tell Joan that he accepted the suggestion and that he thanked her for being willing to help him.

The opportunity came about because Joan had been determined to cover all of London to unearth it. She was happy with her success. She could continue to devote herself to Jim and would probably save him from the claws of winter.

Dick, having been granted a week's leave, had forewarned his grandfather of his arrival. The old man, who was waiting for him on the platform station, welcomed him warmly. Arm-in-arm, the two men climbed into the waiting coupé.

"Dick my boy, what have you decided?" he asked anxiously. "Quick, tell me."

"Well, Sir," said the one-armed veteran, "if you want me, I'll stay with you. But don't forget that I have to be transplanted with care. I'm used to a life that scarcely resembles the one you are offering me. You'll indulge me, but I'm somewhat of a wild plant."

"All right, my dear boy, you'll see you'll be able to do it. You can keep your cherished freedom. I'll not annoy you with societal duties for I live quite retired myself, seeing the outside world only rarely. Do you like books like your father used to?"

"Well yes, I never have enough of them."

"You have a library of five thousand volumes at your disposal. There are books for every taste. If you love life in the outdoors, you can hunt. We have a lot of rabbits here."

Dick couldn't help smiling. "These last years, my occupation was a rabbit trapper. In Australia, you are paid to kill them while a lot of money is spent here keeping them!"

Looking straight into his grandson's eyes the old man suddenly asked: "Do you … do you like whisky?"

Without flinching, the soldier replied simply: "I have never been drunk in my life. I have never drunk more than to quench my thirst. Thank God! My father often warned me about drink. How many times did he say to me: 'In Australia a man who doesn't drink or play has all the luck a man can have. He must be jinxed not to make good his way'."

"That's good, my boy," said the grandfather.

Dick went around the house, the park and the entire property. He saw his father's room as he had left it twenty-four years before. The dust had always been carefully removed. The windows had often been opened to the air of the park, but the furniture, the wallpaper and a few ornaments seemed to reveal that life had stopped in this bedroom long ago. In an old fashioned frame, he saw faded photographs of school groups. His father wearing cricket flannels or riding his favourite pony he had often spoken of. A small book cupboard containing books he loved the most and which he had very often yearned for. The complete works of Shakespeare, Dickens, Byron and even adventure books that had been his first companions. Dick asked that the room stay unoccupied and accepted a room next to it as his room.

The garden, the tall trees, the stables and the huge glass hothouses in which enormous grapes were ripening, everything was full of memories of his father who seemed to follow his footsteps, like a familiar friendly ghost.

Dick found it hard to get used to the sight of all the furniture: the tables, armchairs, gold picture frames, the copper of the fireplaces, the mirrors that everywhere repeated his movements, making him feel a sense of shame. All this luxury seemed to him like a theatre backdrop in the middle of which he was playing the long lost child returning to the fold.

Ancestor and grandson talked for many long hours. Dick recounted, in detail, all he knew of his father's life in Australia and spoke of what he remembered about his mother. The grandfather narrated stories of his son's childhood and Bernard seemed at times to be sitting with them, looking at the flames in the fireplace.

Dick rediscovered the same tongues of fire that had often spoken to him, flames that provided company for him of an evening in the bush. This evening, they contained a strange dream: he was living under a roof that was his, he who had owned only the calico tent that barely hid the moon and the stars from him.

This first evening spent together brought them closer to one another. Dick saw how much his grandfather had suffered, how much he had loved and felt sorry for the son who had left home. He understood that, if both of them could relive those few seconds during which their pride and their wills had locked deeply like the horns of two deer ready to fight to the death, they would not have throw away to the wind twenty years of their lives.

It was late when they rose to say goodnight. The ancestor placed his hands on Dick's shoulders and said: "My child, thank you for coming here, for being willing to stay with me. To give a little of your youth to my old age is a good act and I know our dear Bernard would approve. I don't know how many years I have left, but I want to use them to help you to be happy. I cannot forget the years that have separated us and, later, if you wish, nothing will prevent you undertaking a short trip back to Australia. Sleep well, Dick."

Dick climbed the thick carpeted staircase and entered his bedroom that was brilliantly lit. His room! He turned around several times, went to the huge mirror and spoke to the face looking at him: "Dick, have you been drinking?" And Dick replied: "Don't be an idiot, get undressed and go to bed." He did what he said and got into the soft bed where he momentarily thought he was going to sink down into and disappear. He was too tired from the emotions of the day to put much order into the thoughts that assailed him and suddenly fell asleep.

The next morning, he noticed a shadow crossing his room which was still in the semi-darkness of the drawn curtains. It seized his clothes and left silently. He was going to get up and run after the man when he remembered that this shadow was his personal valet.

Then Dick woke up completely and burst out laughing. He had a valet. What would they say at the store in Boolcara where he sold his rabbit skins! He who had slept fully dressed in a tent nearly all his life. He had a valet who brushed his clothes each morning. Suddenly, he thought out loud: "Provided he doesn't break my pipe which I left in one of my pockets!"

The man returned with the clothes and placed them carefully on the back of a chair and said: "Sir's bath is ready, Sir. Will I show Sir his bathroom?"

Dick got up and followed his valet's fine old-world monkey head, protruding out of his immaculate false collar. When he was immersed up to his neck in the water, he said to himself that he had spent moments in his life that were indeed more disagreeable than these.

CHAPTER XIII

The ship carried about five hundred wounded, broken and nervous men – the flotsam and jetsam from Gallipoli, Flanders and Egypt. Those having lost one arm were grateful to be able to strike a match on a box held tightly between their knees, happy to find, each day, a new ingenious trick to stuff a pipe, or put butter on their bread. Those who had lost a lower limb still considered themselves among the lucky ones, even though the ship's bridge often presented another dangerous place for their balance. The most to be pitied, after the crippled who had to rely on the help of another person, were the internally injured, those who the rigorous European winter or gas had troubled their lungs – those who had what was called the 'civil disease' that caused so much suffering but no glory.

In spite of this, they all hoped to see their country again soon and this thought gave them a strange feeling of bliss they couldn't remember having felt since early childhood. Every now and then, their voices quivered and tears came to their eyes when they thought of the moment the ship would come up alongside the wharf and they would walk down the gangplank. Jim was the only blind person on board and quickly became everyone's spoilt child, so much so that the other nurses seemed to be willing to argue with Joan for the right to be his nurse.

A few of the nurses had already been in the South African campaign, in the Balkans War and the war in Manchuria. One of them, an Australian, had been torpedoed in the Mediterranean three weeks before. It didn't stop her coming back on board another ship as soon as she could. Since that time, she was obsessed, so it seemed, with keeping her safety jacket on every morning when she went to have her shower. Some of these women had been on board different ships for two years, going between England, Egypt and Australia, without thinking of the possibility of encountering more danger than if they were in a hospital under great demand in Nice or Cannes.

Navigation took place with all lights turned off. The number of men on look-out at night was doubled. They saw a periscope in the smallest cork float torn from a fishing line. They also saw – and this was no illusion – cabin doors, crates and wood drifting. They sailed very close past mines. They noticed a whale boat floating along with the current, carrying a crew of seven men who would no longer be tormented by anything in this world.

The idea that they could, from one moment to the next, go down to the deep, or be thrown high in the direction of the firmament, prevented serenity to reign. Nevertheless, they whistled and joked, but each man thought a little more than they would normally do on board that the skin of a boat is quite thin and easily broken.

When they came to the African coast, however, the warm sun helped them forget the night watches and the grey, anxious days they had just been through.

At Port Said where no one was able to get off the ship, the men took pleasure in basking on deck in the sunshine, whose warm caresses they were yearning for like those of a newly-found lost lover. Like the others, Jim took off his tunic, rolled up his sleeves and, with his hat on his head, sat under an avalanche of sunshine. After the Suez Canal in the Red Sea, they had all regained their suntan, which was natural for them as outdoors men, but which they had lost in the continuous rain in Flanders or in the London fog.

"Nurse Joan," said Jim, "this is the first time you've had a taste of real sun. This is real, it caresses and it bites. It reminds you that we are getting closer to it."

"Yes, Jim, I'm beginning to be the same colour as your gaiters and you are browning up right before my eyes."

"And it's not too soon. I felt I was becoming the colour of a lettuce left in a cave."

"It suits you." said Joan. "It suits all the men. I understand now an announcement I read more than once in London: Beautiful bronze skin, without danger, 2/6 a bottle."

"Really?" asked Jim incredulously.

"Yes, it's true," said Joan.

"Well, I'll be hanged!" said Jim shaking his head. "The fact is the London sun, from what I've been told, wouldn't ripen a gooseberry in two summers!"

The blind man stood up and took Joan to the support rail. "On the voyage out," he said, "I stayed hours leaning on the teak rail, looking at the blue and green path we were leaving behind us, or following the flights of the flying fish doing brilliant long ricochets. Nurse Joan, tell me what you can see now."

"Well Jim, the water is such a deep blue it has a giddying effect. It's the colour of lapis lazuli with streaks of silver and large crystal smears running through it. Beautiful dreams must be this colour. The water is broken apart by our boat, cutting it at first and sending fragments right and left. Then it is battered by the two propellers stirring up white foam. After we go on, the blue surface closes up and the large boat is only a memory, leaving no trace, nothing to recall it ever existed... It is so like our lives, Jim – the struggle, the din, every effort, all hits water only. We pass by and we are gone, the earth and man forget that we lived when the earth's large surface closes over us."

Joan saw a big change come over Jim. The sun, his cherished sun had perked him up, his cough had disappeared as if by a spell. But in spite of this, she could feel there was a sadness hiding behind the energy that had him pacing up and down the bridge on a mate's arm. He liked to have her close to him. She dedicated her free time to him. He asked her to read. He preferred reading and was less ready to engage in chatting as he had liked so much before.

While she read aloud, she more than once noticed that his mind was elsewhere. She proved it by rereading the same page straight off. The personal friendship that existed between them slowly disappeared. Jim seemed willing to distance himself from the nurse a little more each day, as if he was getting ready for a complete separation.

When they disembarked, Joan thought she would be happy to see a more reasonable Jim. She had not forgotten what Dick had told her, nor the way he had looked at her. She hoped the idea of seeing his country and his parents again would make the blind man forget this attachment he believed he had for her. She had no illusions. She feared the moment when she would have to say goodbye. She had become for him a gentle habit that would be painful to break all at once.

She noticed he spoke more willingly with the other nurses than with her. In spite of this, he was impatient when she was slow in coming to sit near his deck chair. Joan was a woman, a woman could not help seeing Jim suffer in silence and that he tried, by every means possible, to hide the cause of his suffering. Joan thought that this suffering had to be profound and the idea of suffering in a place that was dark and more sombre than the darkest of nights frightened her.

They had to stay twenty-four hours in Colombo to take on coal. Jim had invitations from everyone wanting to look after him and take him ashore. But he wanted to stay faithful to Joan and Joan was happy about that. After they disembarked, she took him by car to Mount Lavinia.

On the shore lined with coconut trees, they listened to the sea washing onto the sand in catlike bounds and retreating gently, making a noise like spilling pearls by the bushel.

An Indian performed a miracle in front of them with a germinating mango seed. It grew and within a few seconds became a very healthy green bush. The Indian let Jim touch the dried out mango seed, then the delicate stem of the green leaves of the young tree. The blind man held in his hands precious stones that had been shaped into marbles from soda bottles and heard Joan haggle over toys that were, at first, worth a fabulous amount of rupees, but whose price tumbled dangerously down close to a half-crown. Jim was agreeably surprised to discover that he still enjoyed a lot of things despite his lack of sight. His remaining senses told him distinctly that he was in Colombo: the smell of ripe fruit, wood that burnt giving off a bitter and sometimes strangely perfumed smoke, the smell of thousands of tiny dishes containing all types of fried food warming on fires in the open air. He heard the rustling of coconut palms and bamboo, the chant of strolling merchants, the groaning of cart wheels, the cry of the rickshaw drivers who passed by, out of breath. In the hotel dining room, he could make out bare feet tapping on the parquet floor, the noise on the mats while he felt with sheer delight the breeze from the ceiling fans caress his hair.

After lunch, Joan lead him again under the coconut palms. They sat on an old upturned catamaran that was chipped like an old piece of pottery. They enjoyed listening to the tiny beggars who formed a circle around them.

"Do you want a guide?" one asked.

"Post cards?" tried another.

"Do a cartwheel?" said a third.

And in their pidgin English, they all offered something to buy, false stamps, a snake skin or a small model of an outrigger. Finally, Joan sent them away by saying, "No more money", and the last ones were chased away by an umbrella. At a respectable distance, small bronze statues danced like crazy puppets, showing white teeth and crying as they twisted: "No more money!"

A woman passed nearby with her child and Joan beckoned to her. She moved graciously closer. The music of her silver ankle bracelets, as they struck together, made her movements even more beautiful. She smiled, happy to show them the child she was carrying on her left hip. While Joan took the small brown hand that seized her finger, the mother saw that, under the stark shade of his hat, the man's eyes were closed. Then she noticed on Jim's left sleeve the bar with golden stripes. She knew what it was. She had been told it was what the king gave to his fighters for each wound.

The Sinhalese woman placed her free hand on his eyes, then, worried, looked at Joan. She was asking a question. Joan nodded and placed her own hand in front of her eyes to convey what had happened. The woman seemed to forget the child who was playing with Joan's chain. Her smile slipped from her face and, in her big limpid eyes, the nurse suddenly saw a deep despair where there had been pity, sympathy and something more that she had not understand at first. She was then able to read, for the first time, the deep maternal love that filled the dark pupils of these Oriental women – a maternal love that seemed to have been there for centuries, since the beginning of time, as if to prove that these races were indeed the mothers of the whole of humanity.

The woman held her child closer, looked at the blind man and offered him her child's chubby hand. Joan guided Jim's hand. He took the tiny hand and kissed it. Her large, dark eyes once again were fixed on Joan. Joan understood this second question: "Is this your man?"

Without hesitating, Joan nodded, "yes".

The Sinhalese looked at her and Joan knew that the look meant: Be three times blessed for being his wife, his mother and his sister. The nurse watched the woman go away, holding her crying child close to her chest.

"I can hear her anklets like small sad bells going off in the distance," said Jim.

"No … not sad," Joan added thoughtfully.

Jim filled his pipe. Sitting next to him, Joan was looking, but not seeing the blue and white waves come and go on the sand at the foot of the coconut palms. She had just had a lesson in charity, sympathy and love. The Sinhalese woman had shown her that the blind man deserved all that. She, so good, so devoted, she wondered if she had given enough of herself, if she had not been selfish.

She had replied 'yes' to the second question, her nod wanted to say, "Yes, I am his spouse". She knew, at that very second, that she had promised her life to Jim. She would offer him her life before the sun set that day.

An hour later, they were in the cinnamon garden. The evening was very beautiful, filled with strange perfumes. The large trees heavy with clusters of white flowers were everywhere in the middle of noisy bamboo and dishevelled palm trees. Joan thanked fate for having brought her into this earthly paradise. After a moment of silence and with her heart racing, she said: "Jim, do you want me … do you want me to be your wife?"

Jim grabbed her into his arms and asked in a husky voice: "Did I hear you correctly, Joan?"

But Joan did not want to repeat the question. Moreover, she couldn't as Jim's lips were on hers.

CHAPTER XIV

The bay of Sydney is a wonder. Australians claim that it is the most beautiful in the world. Don't tell them that the bay of Rio de Janeiro is even more beautiful and more grandiose. You would cause them pain and they would not believe you. Remember that, when you go to the Antipodes, don't knock their harbour. Sydneyites would never forgive you.

An hour before the ship was about to enter the harbour through the heads, everyone was on the deck anxious to disembark. Standing under the gangway, Joan was looking at the raised, rocky coastline which was not at all welcoming. Jim recounted the story of the *Dunbar* which had missed the entrance in 1867 deceived by the lights they had noticed above an indentation in the cliff face. The *Dunbar* was turned into fragments at the foot of the rock face.

When Joan saw the ship change direction and enter the large opening which was the entry to the port, she felt she was penetrating a new world where a new life for her was about to begin. A little later, when Jim felt the ground at Circular Quay under his feet, he squeezed his fiancée's arm and said: "Dear Joan, may Australia be good to you! Welcome."

They stayed in Sydney briefly, taking the country train the same evening.

Joan saw the countryside they were travelling through at first light the following day. From that moment, she loved the wide plain, unravelling endlessly before their eyes, the flocks of animals that fled as the train approached and the horses that galloped by. She looked at the small dwellings with their tiny gardens, as they rose at rare intervals in the midst of a bunch of trees like an island lost in this ocean of yellow grass. It was December and the height of summer. The rivers and creeks they passed were low and they soon felt the strength of the sun.

Jim answered the myriad questions Joan asked. A man on horseback, followed by a dozen dogs, made them think of Dick who had stayed back with his grandfather. The man waved his arm to thank them for the bundle of newspapers thrown out to him from one of the doors. She understood what the two bearded walkers were following the rail line and carrying on their backs a large bundle rolled in a blanket, with a billy in one hand and a sailcloth bag in the other containing their water supply. She quickly recognised them as 'swaggies' who Jim had often spoken about.

Actually, Jim saw everything through Joan's eyes. Every now and then, they stopped at a country platform where very few people were waiting. Bags containing mail, a sewing machine, a cart or a machine to poison rabbits were unloaded. Then the train set off again along the line that went on to infinity, along the pink plain which seemed endless.

They were coming to the station where they had to get off. Jim wanted to be standing at the door of the carriage, but stayed in his corner, nervous and emotional. The train finally stopped. Joan helped Jim get off. Suddenly, he felt arms surrounding him tight and he recognised his father's voice, his father's rough voice saying: "My boy," but he couldn't say more.

Jim could only say "Dad" and responded to the embrace. Then he found words and said: "Dad, this is my fiancée who has brought me back home."

And Bill, somewhat shy in front of this strange woman, shook her hand and said: "Bless you, Miss. You are welcome."

Friends surrounded Jim. He felt hands squeezing his and seizing his broad shoulders. Joan took his father to one side with the pretext of getting the luggage standing on the platform and said softly to him: "Show how happy you are to see him again without letting him guess any sign of sadness. His misfortune is great, but we are here to help him forget. I believe he is as happy as he can be."

They packed the luggage onto a buggy drawn by two horses, tied it securely for the trip that would take two hours. Jim stroked the horses, placed his hand on the shoulder of the one on the left and patted it for a while. "Dad," he shouted, "a C in a circle. It's Sultan!"

"It is," said his father. "And the other one?"

Jim lightly touched the other horse and said: "Of course, it's Sam. He's the only one with such sensitive skin. He shakes his leather if a fly lands six yards from him. Good old Sam!"

The road seemed short. Father and son had so much to say to each other. Joan had so much to see. In the evening, they stopped at a station where they and the horses spent the night. Joan was touched to see how each person was good to Jim and her, a stranger, as if they had known her for years. The frank hospitality was sincere and put her at ease from the very first.

After dinner, chairs were taken into the garden and the first evening was spent under the vast Australian starry sky and Joan was most impressed. The noises of the bush were new to her. She could recognise the croaking of the frogs that formed an incessant monotonous bass that was not disagreeable. From time to time, a cry rose in the night along the river, something that resembled barking, the cry of the mopoke. Later, there was the call of the curlew, a very sad sound like the cry of someone lost. The flowers in the garden invaded the air as if bottles of perfume had been spilled and there was a surreal calm that seemed to belong to another world. Despite the fatigue of the long day, they went to bed late so they could enjoy the beautiful night as long as possible.

The next day, the buggy left early and it was nearly sunset before the carriage stopped in front of the small cottage on *Lone Man Plain*.

The poor mother, who had been waiting hours for them, heard the horses' hooves, but didn't dare come out of the dwelling. Every member of her body was trembling with joy and a strange fear she could not explain. She would have fallen, if her son's arms had not held her. At first, she saw the dark glasses. Then, she noticed Joan holding a finger to her lips, as a signal to her, her wide eyes pleading. She understood and her arms held her son more tightly. Large tears streamed down her face, brought on by a deep feeling of joy and a very sudden acute sadness.

Joan took Jim's hand and he introduced his fiancée to his mother who, kissing her future daughter-in-law, said with a smile: "Jim, my boy, you have chosen well. I believe she is as good as she is sweet to look at. We will try to make her like us as well."

During the simple evening meal, Jim was the happiest of them all. Sitting next to his mother, he showed her to put the salt for him at the top of his plate and the mustard at the bottom, that is the salt at midday and the mustard at six o'clock, as they said at St-Dunstan's.

"Mother," he added, "we are going to raise chickens. We will have hens that will lay like silkworms. We are going to make fine small huts for them and it will keep me busy. We won't be frightened by crows or iguanas as we'll put a fence all around."

He went on developing his plans for a long time. Everyone was happy to see him looking so courageously to the future.

On the veranda his father offered him tobacco. He started to cut small shavings before rolling them to fill his pipe. For an hour, he listened to what had been done at *Lone Man Plain* during his absence. Wells had been dug and windmills erected. They had planted thirty acres of luzern grass along the river's edge, an experiment expected to give good results.

When Joan had finished helping his mother clear the table and do the washing up, Jim asked her to give him the lamp for he wanted to light it himself to show her the walls of the dining room.

"Tell me what you see," said Jim.

"There's a polar landscape with bears, seals and icebergs," she replied. "Next to it is a caravan of lamas coming down a road in the Andes; beside that is the Egyptian desert and pyramids…"

"I really would like to see this large scene again as it was one of the last I was able to see. After that the blind fell, a very heavy blind which will never again go up!"

"Here," said Joan, to distract his dark thoughts a little, "is a view of Hyde Park. The people are dressed in the fashion of the … where is the date of the newspaper? … the 1880s."

"Just think, that all my childhood I dreamt of getting to know the streets where Dickens' characters lived, the country where Walter Scott's men and women fought and loved; the country where my grandparents were born. It could be said that an evil fairy answered my childhood wishes, but she took away my sight … Joan, you don't know what you've done for me, to make me love life again. There were moments in London and on the boat when I considered my life like a rag only worth throwing away and certainly not worth the effort of picking it up. I hope you didn't listen too carefully to your feelings of pity, Joan and that your love for me isn't just your deep charitable self. Sometimes, I am frightened by the extent of your sacrifice."

"Jim, you know quite well that I know there is so much future happiness for me in loving you and becoming your wife to call it a sacrifice."

"Mother," Jim said when he had resumed his seat on the veranda, "you should consider yourself a happy mother for there will be a lot who will continue hopelessly waiting for their boys, until they take their last breath. In Egypt, in Gallipoli and in France, they are many who sleep beneath a small wooden cross and each cross will testify to people over there that we from downunder knew how to fight for a noble idea."

The next day, the boss arrived with his wife in his buggy to see Jim and his fiancée.

The wedding ceremony was fixed for Christmas Eve. The boss and his wife asked that it be held at the homestead so that everyone on *Lone Man Plain* could be there. Jim and Joan received their first wedding present – a paper duly signed giving them right to choose a piece of land along the creek or the river. Jim thanked the boss and together he and Joan chose land on the creek. *Lone Man Plain* also gave them essential building material and helping hands to construct a cottage.

One evening the following week, Jim was the first to hear the sound of harnessed horses coming in their direction. Soon after, Joan drove him close to the creek where they could hear voices talking to horses impatient to be unharnessed. A man approached and said simply: "Good evening." He took Jim's hand and shook it.

"Peter, it's you," said the blind man. "I recognise your voice."

"Yes, Jim, it's me. I'm happy to see you here again. We're bringing you and unloading your house, the walls, roofing, floor boards, every-thing is here. Tomorrow at daylight Jim you will hear your home grow."

He turned to Joan and said: "Good evening Miss, we all wish you a warm welcome to *Lone Man Plain* because you brought Jim back to us."

After placing the equipment carefully in a pile, the men, who came with the harnessed cart and horses, lit a fire and put up a tent near the creek. Peter led Jim and Joan close to the fire, made them sit on a tree trunk and they talked for a long time drinking tea.

At the break of dawn, Jim got up and, alone, he followed the path in the middle of the tall grass. The men had already started digging holes for the blocks of pine already prepared for the house foundations. By the evening, the blocks were in place. Jim and Joan sat on two of them, as if they were taking possession of their dwelling.

The homestead carpenter who had mortised all the wood in advance arrived the next day. Jim recognised his first blows with the hammer and went to shake his hand. As Peter had told him, he heard his house growing. At first, it was the muffled blows that joined the mortises and the supports. Later, they were the singing blows whose levels rose as the men hammered five-inch nails into the wood. When the frame was up, Jim could make out the huge crate filled with corrugated iron that thundered as it was fixed to make the walls and the roof. The men worked as best as they could; they worked well and fast for Jim and his future wife.

On the fourth day, Jim said to Joan: "Come and see the house."

They went in by one of the openings without doors or windows and walked through the three bedrooms of the dwelling. One man was busy building the fireplaces. Jim was pleased to smell cement and damp plaster that suggested to him the freshness of a cellar. Joan thought her cottage was like a brand new toy. The smell of fresh pine added to this sensation. She loved the natural simplicity of the dwelling that was going to encompass her new existence. She loved the verandas where they could talk in the dark evenings.

Two days before the wedding, Joan let Jim and his parents finish what needed to be done to the house and went to the homestead where she was the guest of the boss and his wife. She went out several times with the boss in his buggy, accompanying him on his long rounds of the station's paddocks. During this time, Mrs Mills made the most of their absences to practise the harmonium and patiently and zealously study two hymns and a wedding march which was not Wagner's.

The chosen clergyman arrived twenty-four hours before the ceremony. He was the same man who had baptised Jim with water from Parrot Creek twenty years earlier.

The homestead dining room had been decorated with flowers and garlands made from the branches of orange trees and peppercorn trees. Everything that could be taken from the garden found a place in the room. The double doors of the dining room had to be opened because all the people of *Lone Man Plain* wanted to be present at Jim's marriage. The old Chinese gardener, anxious to take his place among the guests, had dressed in his special clothes.

Dressed in a simple tailored dress, Joan promised to be faithful to Jim and to be with him in 'happy times and difficult ones'.

When they had shaken hands with everyone and thanked them for the gifts which *Lone Man Plain* had showered on them, the married couple left in a buggy for the creek where their home was waiting for them. They got there a little before sunset. The pale blue sky was waning in a large golden mist.

"Dear Jim," said Joan before going inside their cottage, "may our small home be blessed. May its walls and roof hold much happiness."

And Jim replied: "What I have given for the old country, I do not regret. The old country has well and truly paid me back."

SHORT STORIES

The Grey House[1]

London was terribly sad on this particular morning in February.
From an unseen sky fell a constant slow rain, a rain that seemed to
date from the Flood desiring to continue till the end of the world. This
same morning, Private Tucker, 6030 of the Australian Imperial Force,
saw life through a fog that engulfed his entire being. He felt that all the
tears of all the eyes on earth were falling on him. Sitting on a bench and
shivering in his overcoat, he was alone. His felt hat was heavy and the
drops of water flowed over its edges with each movement he made. His
head was heavy. He knew his thoughts were messed up and shattered
like a boat cabin after a tempest.

He had just woken up. His memory tried, as best it could, to swim
against a powerfully strong current. He asked himself for the fourth time
how he had been shipwrecked on a lonely bench in Hyde Park. Then
he remembered that he had been upturned and buried on the Somme
where he had come from. The first thing he did, after struggling out,
had been to touch himself to see if anything was broken. It seemed as if
something had swallowed him. The left pocket of his jacket was empty.
His wallet had disappeared.

He began to comprehend. He straightened up and tried to remember. Yesterday was vague and seemed a long time ago. Yesterday, he
had dined in a restaurant in Piccadilly. A man came to his small table
and politely asked if he could sit at the place opposite. The stranger
knew Australia. He spoke about Bourke, Sydney and Melbourne. He
even described his descent into the Star of the East, a gold mine in
Ballarat. He offered him a cigar. In return, Tucker offered him a crème
de menthe and, after chatting a while, they went to the Coliseum, each
paying his own way. They went into a bar for a whisky before it closed.
Tucker remembered the lights of Piccadilly Circus, taxis going by,
buses almost touching them as they passed – huge beasts trying not to

harm anyone. He suddenly felt as if the earth was giving away beneath the soles of his feet. And then he remembered nothing else.

It was still raining. Tucker was cold and hungry. He was ashamed of having been duped by the stranger. He had been warned of the dangers Australians faced in London. He had been told there were men and women lying in wait the moment he stepped onto Waterloo or Charing Cross station for they knew a soldier wearing a soft hat with its brim turned up over the left ear was paid the wage of a lieutenant and was endowed with princely generosity.

He had been careful and hadn't had anything to do with strangers. He had even gone as far as telling charitable souls who wanted to explain Westminster Abbey to him or guide him through the Tower to go to hell. Alone, a small book in hand, he saw St Paul's, the city and the grey Thames that appeared like a sea in the mysterious fog. He had gone to theatres; seen stupid revues that made you cry; listened to ordinary music. But he had enjoyed himself. The armchairs were most comfortable and you could smoke as much as you liked.

Over in France, he had seen sad things. He heard sounds that tore at your soul and twisted every muscle. Here, he felt as if he were a child again frightened by the surroundings, abandoned as the sea encircles a person shipwrecked on a small deserted arid island. He was alarmed by the cruel solitude in this grey London – a solitude that seemed more absolute than the one he had once experienced when he was lost out west on the Kangaroo Plain where he stayed three days without food or drink. Around him, the trees rustled, their bare black trunks shining in the fog like sea lions emerging from the water. His watch had disappeared. He didn't know what time it was. There were very few people passing by and they all seemed in a hurry. Opposite him on the other side of Park Lane, he was struck by a house. He had a vague notion he had seen it somewhere in a dream or in a book. It was made of carved stone; all the windows were small, ribbed, with lead mesh. It seemed to belong neither to the London he knew, nor to the present.

So where had he seen this house before?

He felt himself being carried away at speed in a huge cloud of dust, beneath a blinding sun. And suddenly, he was at Tartana Downs in the mining area of North Queensland ... far from Hyde Park. He knew this was a dream house, but in Queensland where he had seen it for the first time. He was sure of it now. Yes. One day near the homestead of Tartana Downs, he had picked up a picture book that one of his boss's children had lost. He had hidden it under his shirt and had taken it back to camp where he looked at it all night, even in the glow from the fire. The following week, he had given the book back to his boss.

Again and again, he had read the story of the Fairy who lived in the Grey House and who invited all unhappy passersby to come in. He remembered the image of the house, the stone entrance worn down by the feet of the people who had come to see the Fairy.

That's when the strange dream started. Near him a bare-headed man, in a long black mackintosh and holding an umbrella, took him by the arm and dragged him away. Tucker didn't have the energy to resist, but he wanted to laugh as the man was holding the umbrella open over his head. Tucker had never been under an umbrella. He had never ever owned an umbrella. They left the park through the gate, crossed the road and went towards the Grey House. The man opened the large carved oak door with a tiny key and, just as shown in the picture book, the door had heavy black hinges.

The first thing he saw in the hall was the fire burning in the fire-place. He headed straight for the hearth with his hands outstretched, his legs apart, giving himself completely to its warmth which was as sweet and charitable as a mother. His companion pushed a large chair behind him, but Tucker remained standing as if he were looking to embrace or caress a long lost friend, an old mate from many a solitary camp downunder, in Australia.

The man, who brought him here, had a ruddy round face. He seemed good and, as he removed his overcoat, asked him if he wasn't too damp.

What a strange dream! Never had anyone helped him take his coat off! Tucker told him what had happened to him. He felt shame that he had been duped, but indignation is stronger than shame and it did him good to be able to tell someone that fourteen pounds sterling had been stolen from him. It wasn't the money that shook him, but the idea of having been taken down by another.

The man brought him some Bovril and biscuits on a tray. Tucker accepted all the more willingly as he learnt that breakfast would be ready in half an hour. He sat in a large armchair. He had never seen or tried such a chair. He ate and drank and looked blissfully at the steam rising from the soles of his shoes.

The stranger signalled him to follow. He led him to a large bowl filled with hot water. Tucker admired the white marble washstand. There were mirrors everywhere, new bars of soap that smelt good and soft thick towels. He took off his jacket, rolled up his sleeves, opened his collar and gave himself a really good wash. He put his head into the basin several times that allowed him, soon after doing so, to use a brush and comb and make a perfectly straight part.

A new Tucker emerged from the room. He felt he had washed away the ill-fated night. He stood again in front of the fire. The man told him ceremoniously that Lady Sybil was in the dining room waiting for him to join her for breakfast. He was suddenly frightened ... Lady Sybil was the "fairy" in the Grey House... He had never spoken to a "fairy", but the word breakfast gave him courage for he was as hungry as a dingo. With both hands, he pulled the bottom of his uniform jacket to adjust it. And with his best Australian appearance of both horseman and sailor, he entered the large dining room.

A small girl dressed in white came to meet him. She held out her hand and asked him if James had looked after him and given him what he needed. Tucker felt at ease. The "fairy" was so young, so sweet and so natural. She was also very tactful, at least that was Tucker's impression, for she filled a large coffee cup for him and insisted he start eating his porridge. She said grace and the soldier, who had looked long and hard at the table covered with all sorts of things, mentally added a *post scriptum* after the Amen, fervently asking the good Lord not to stop this beautiful dream in the middle as always happened with his good dreams.

He had never dreamed, sleeping or awake, of such a breakfast. There were two spoons, two forks and three knives either side of his plate. At first, he wondered if he would use all of them. James brought him an extra knife and fork to eat the magnificent apples.

"When I got up this morning," said Lady Sybil, as she poured a second cup of coffee, "I saw you sitting on a seat in Hyde Park opposite here. I rang for the maid and asked her to send James to fetch you. Today is my sixteenth birthday. Mum asked me yesterday, before she left on her trip, what I wanted for my party. I said: Not money, no presents, but simply the permission to do what I would like all day long. Mum hesitated a little, but since I'm not a very terrible person, she agreed."

"So the first thing I did was to give Miss Crawford a day off and sent her home to her family. She needed it and so did I. Miss Crawford is my governess, a woman who, as Mum has said, has very outstanding qualities. She is good and knows a lot. Unfortunately, she hates words and expressions such as 'ripping' or 'topping'. If she were here, I believe she would not have allowed me to invite you to come in, because we haven't been introduced!... When does your leave end?"

"I have to be at Waterloo Station this evening at 7.30," Tucker said.

"What a pity it is so short. We will try to have you spend the day as pleasantly as possible. Do you have to go out? To do some shopping before leaving?"

The soldier said very simply that he had no need to buy anything, thinking that the nine pence still in his pocket wouldn't go far. He also admitted that a morning spent in a theatre wouldn't make him smile much. So it was decided that they would stay quietly in the house.

Added to this was the fact that it had not stopped raining and, looking at the sky, it seemed there was more for another month or two.

Lady Sybil showed him the way to the smoking room where she sat Tucker in a leather armchair. She offered him a Corona which he smoked casually, thinking of the pipe he would light up after the cigar. She asked all sorts of questions about Australia that Tucker had pleasure in answering. After forty-five minutes, Lady Sybil felt she had learnt more natural history, geography, geology and ethnology than Miss Crawford had ever known. Tucker had actually been a trapper, miner and even a cook for an expedition in Central Australia.

What Miss Crawford knew about Australia, she had learnt in Bond Street in the display windows of three shops that showed opals, apples and several cockatoos as coming from the Antipodes.

The morning passed rapidly and time for lunch came as a surprise to both of them. Tucker seemed to have forgotten the copious breakfast. He allowed himself to be served fine slices of cold meat and he added different pickles from an amazing choice. James filled his glass with stout with an attentive concern. Lady Sybil left him in the smoking room with cigars, cigarettes and illustrated newspapers. Tucker soon succumbed to the repeated offer of the leather chair and felt himself gently falling asleep, sliding from one dream into another.

It was 5 o'clock when the soldier got up, straightened and stretched. James, who had silently followed the progress of his restorative sleep, came and announced that tea was served in the lounge room. Tea was one of those teas Tucker had never seen in real life. He counted three sorts of small cakes, tarts and a marvellous rainbow-coloured cake with layers of green, yellow, pink and white on top of each other. Tucker had three slices for Lady Sybil had told him again to eat well before setting out.

The time to say goodbye came all too soon. Tucker left the Grey House with a heavy heart and was frightened afterwards that he had squeezed Lady Sybil's hand a little too strongly. As she placed a parcel for the road under his arm, she promised to send him something from time to time while he was at the Front.

James also received a warm handshake after helping Tucker put on his large overcoat and get into the Rolls Royce that was to take him to the station. This trip in the padded limousine put a dignified end to a marvellous journey. Tucker would willingly have changed places and sit near the driver, for he felt too important alone in the back of the large car.

Under the cold light of Waterloo Station hall, the dream evaporated like incense smoke that remains in the air for a long time. Men in khaki moved in every direction. The Newfoundlanders in their Scottish kilts, with two large feathers in the caps, rubbed shoulders with soft-skinned Maoris while colonial caps gave a strange note in the cold foggy atmosphere. Fortunately, Tucker still had his leave document and his luggage locker ticket. He took up his bag, his pack, hung his zinc hat on his belt and, in a thoughtful mood, sat on a seat to wait for his train.

He had not left the Grey House. He could still feel its warm hospitality, all the goodness held within its walls. It had been a beautiful dream that would remain with him. It would go to France and, in the trenches of the Somme, he would think often of his young "fairy".

Placing a hand under one of the straps of his pack, Tucker felt something in a pocket inside his overcoat. He fossicked under the pressure of the straps and, with difficulty, brought out a wallet. It wasn't his. It was a brand new doeskin wallet with silver corners. He opened it. One of the pockets contained fourteen pounds sterling; in another, there was a letter written in pencil: 'Make me happy by accepting this. Today is my birthday. Good luck. Lady Sybil'.

And Tucker felt completely awake. He put the wallet in his pocket and shook his shoulder to one side as he picked up his pack and disappeared into the khaki crowd engulfing the platform.

The Blind and the Cripple[2]

It was clear that visitors were not expected in the Hospital X's Joffre Room that afternoon. The laughter was so loud that I scarcely dared enter the ward for fear of spoiling the festivities. Before I was noticed, I saw the wounded sitting on their beds, those convalescing were standing, all were watching the nurse scolding, with all the force she had left after laughing uproariously at Private Henri Ledru, or at least at what remained of this small brave young soldier.

The fun stopped as soon as they noticed me. Some took my Anglo-French Red Cross khaki uniform for an English officer and shouted, "Settle!" while I went to the nurse who was still talking with Ledru.

The hospital had everything it needed, claimed Miss X... Nevertheless, if the London Committee, which had been so generous, could send a few more thermometers, pyjamas, shirts, cotton wool, etc (in fact quite a small list) which I noted as she spoke, the hospital would be very grateful.

I was introduced to the sick men. One had a bullet explode in his leg; another had an arm shattered by shrapnel; another, a head that had been reshaped like a broken soup tureen and now seemed to be as solid as ever. There were all sorts of cases, yet nearly all were well on the way to being healed.

This was the eighty-seventh hospital I had visited and, as usual, I took note of the entrance, the yard, the kitchen areas, the corridors. Everything was scrupulously clean. The staircases and corridors had been washed that morning; the floor of the Joffre Room was like a polished deck of a ship. One very good note for Hospital X.

The nurse had intentionally left introducing Private Ledru until the end. All he had left was his right arm, body and head, but all the force and energy, the will of a strong man, was concentrated in what was still there. I shook his hand and felt the strength that this arm and hand retained of life as strong as iron claws.

'We can do nothing, Sir, since his wounds have healed. He makes others laugh so much they feel sick. He plays rotten tricks and tells stories that make your ribs ache.'

Ledru interrupted her very politely and said: "Major" (they take me for a doctor because I have red crosses on the collar of my vest and one on my cap), "when someone has been changed as I have, you have the right to laugh a little. I was a clown in a Paris circus. When I saw you come in, I was telling them of my plans. No more dangerous jumps for me, no work on a flat saddle or on a steel wire. They sug-gested I could be a crier at Les Halles, a seller of chestnuts or Turkish Delight, a country mailman in Holland in a small boat, you know, with one scull. An aviator's observer. Or ballast for zeppelins, but I can't make up my mind."

It was time for tea. An English nurse had started this fashion in the hospital and it was very much appreciated.

"Do you know the first thing he said when he woke from his third amputation? 'I went in with three and came out with one. Fortunately it's the right one'. The stretcher-bearers wondered how they were going to put this poor creature, who was broken into pieces, on the stretcher. He was complaining atrociously without raising his voice for fear of spreading his pain to others. Fortunately, the ambulance was not far off. The shell responsible for putting Ledru in this condition had doubt-lessly been meant for the building bearing the Red Cross flag. I won't try to explain why or how Ledru didn't die, thus making the major who looked after him proud. I can no more explain how he has kept his good humour – as you've seen – that is continuously flowing like a small stream of clean, refreshing water. We all fear the day when he must leave us. We fear for his future for he has no relatives or friends. We know that this war has given rise everywhere to goodness in all its beauty, as if it wants to make us forget the diabolic horrors it brings about. Ledru is at everyone's mercy like a newborn needing help all the time. I still hope that a dedicated person will be found to help him along the way."

The nurse showed me the way out in order to add one of two things more to the list. As we went past a door, I heard a muffled waltz playing on a gramophone. Stopping before opening the door, the nurse said: "That's a blind man."

In the large room, a Sister of Mercy was sitting at a table near a soldier who wasn't moving as he listened to what the black disk was singing.

"I'm all right", Remy, the blind man told me, "except I would really like to feel the country air. I'm a country boy and I love the woods and the fields. People are good to me. They take me to the town, but I can't hear the wind in the trees or the birds. The yard sparrows are not real birds. They are like the cities' urchins – hardly birds!"

As I was leaving the room, I had an idea. Would it be possible to organise these two lives to be together and be less unhappy, one helping the other? Remy and Ledru – the blind and the cripple!

I told the nurse. She agreed it would probably work and was worth trying. We thought Remy would not have too many difficulties. He was strong and it would be easy for him to push a wheelchair which Henri would steer with his remaining hand. She agreed. They would try it. A male nurse brought Henri into the office and sat him in the armchair. The suggestion was put before him, slowly, one point at a time.

Did he like the country?

"Oh, yes", he said. "I'm saving my money to set myself up later somewhere on my own piece of land, about an acre. Well, a square yard would be enough." Seeing him made you forget his misfortune. Both the nurse and I burst out laughing. He said he liked Remy not only because he was blind, but he was a good chap, a brave soldier.

"*M'sieur le Major*, I believe that the idea is full of promise. Remy can push me and I will guide him. We will be a family together, we'll go to the market and we'll remain good mates for sure, seeing we cannot go anywhere without the other. Except, *M'sieur le Major*, I'm not yet free, no legs, one arm. I have already written several times, but have received no answer. I don't know if they intend to find me a place in a submarine, or I could work the wireless for the war effort. It could be said they have trouble letting me go."

A fortnight later, the London Committee of the French Red Cross received a letter from the nurse at Hospital X:

> The arrival of the wheelchair you so generously sent us has been a triumph. Ledru and Remy had to make a tour of the hospital, what Ledru called a 'trial gallop'. The two brave men were delighted. They went into the street and the outing was most successful. Both men were like children trying out a new toy. It gave Ledru a baroque idea. He asked for a pair of shoes from the store. Not seeing any pressing need for these luxury items for Ledru, the store refused his request. So I gave Ledru money to buy what he needed. He came back with a pair of legs with the feet shod with clumpy new shoes. He found a way to stuff a pair of canvas combat trousers with packing straw which, under the blanket, completed the illusion as his new shoes were seen looking as natural as the real thing.

In a letter that was enclosed, Ledru took it upon himself to thank the Committee on behalf of them both:

> My friend Remy and I don't know how to show our gratitude. The only thing we can say is that it's worthwhile being maimed and even killed to find brave people in our countries.

> PS We have already received several letters from different parts of France offering us board and lodgings. It makes us cry to find how kind people are.

Corporal Jones[3]

Corporal Jones of the Sussex Regiment had fought well. That he talked too much was the only thing that could be said against him. He boasted of what he had done *and* of what he had not done. The Boches he had killed, either by laying them low by rifle, or by thrusting them through with his bayonet, had already numbered a dozen. His companions began to complain that in the trenches, there was too much noise from Jones. They could hear only him.

After a week at the Front, they went to the back for a short rest. The corporal and four men had the task of unpacking a consignment of provisions that had arrived directly from London. Everyone knew that the Tommies were well fed. You were easily convinced of this, when you saw what was in each of the cases: tea, bacon, marmalade, biscuits, all this seemed to us *poilus* [French soldiers] to be luxury food. Tommy thought of them as absolutely necessary items.

As it was being unloaded, a large case marked 'Huntley and Palmer' so very unfortunately fell on Corporal Jones' knee and he had to be taken to hospital straightaway. An exposed nail added to the injury causing the wound to be just as serious and painful as any caused by shrapnel. Jones suffered doubly, because his pride had also been deeply wounded.

Like all conceited men, he was extremely thin-skinned. He had been in hospital for two days only before he was given the nickname 'Biscuits'. Gibes thrown at him from one bed to the next increased since they knew each comment hit home. Corporal Jones paid for his bragging – dearly. He found biscuit crumbs in his bed; he saw a biscuit beribboned as a war medal on his bedside table and, since all kinds of biscuits were an integral part of the hospital diet, it seemed as though he was caught in a hail of bullets.

Fortunately for Jones after two weeks, he was sent to London to convalesce. His arrival had some effect, although a Cockney is not disposed to get carried away emotionally, even for their heroes. Jones was still limping badly, leaving no doubt of the seriousness of his wound.

His family joyously welcomed him home. They were proud of him when he showed them the bits of bullets and shrapnel that had been removed from his knee. Jones did not do things by half. The colourful stories accompanying this exhibition proved, at least, that the corporal's imagination had not been injured. To help it along, he had a mind for detail that many skites do not, making their triumphs short-lived.

His friends pampered him. He handed out – left and right – bits of shell and shrapnel taken from around his left kneecap. One Sunday, he was strolling in Hyde Park which is the Agora of London:[4] the pulpit, stage and platform for religious maniacs, suffragettes and socialists. There on the day of rest, the crowd found one of the rare distractions. And the people were always numerous. Here, they could hear rhetoric against the devil, the politician, or mankind. To believe any of the speakers, one was no better than the other.

Since the beginning of the war, suffragettes and socialists were quieter and less full of hate, but the devil is always ranted about – especially now with recruitment meetings and their advocates.

Corporal Jones, attracted by the military band, pushed his way into the crowd around the tribune where a young officer was speaking, while waving a cane in his left hand. His right arm was supported by a large black sling. He invited the young men listening to sign enlistment papers not only to defend their country, but also to fight for the cause of justice and freedom.

He thanked the applauding crowd with a wave. A Scottish soldier in a regimental kilt took his place on the dais. He had a great success as a speaker, not just because his humour reminded the listeners of Harry Lauder. He began by telling them that he, personally, had no fear for Scotland. The country had never been conquered and never would be, because nobody wanted it. Moreover, a country in which a Jew couldn't eke out a living was not one to tempt the Germans. He went on, in the same dry way, entertaining the people who had just begun to enjoy themselves a little on a Sunday since the last few years.

Jones' vanity, his need to talk and be heard urged him to the foot of the platform where he said something to the recruiting officer stationed there. When the Scot came down amid flattering comments, the officer announced that Corporal Jones, just returning from the Front, would say a few words. Jones spoke with ease, using familiar rhetorical language which the English use at every level of society – a habit that at times painfully lengthens a dinner party or a meeting of only six people.

"Yes, my friends", he began. "I have come from the Front, where I was wounded in the knee while carrying munitions to the frontline trenches. In a few days, I will be fine, ready to go back. Coming to London the other day, I was astonished to see so many young men in civilian dress. I see them now in the crowd, on my right and on my left. What reason do you have for not wearing the khaki uniform? What don't you like? The colour? The cut? Perhaps it's the low pay? A shilling a day and good food! Do you know what our French allies are paid? Three halfpennies. Yes, they do – that's what you pay for a small beer. And you know as well as I do that they get themselves killed for that price. They don't bargain!"

Once started, Corporal Jones went on for twenty minutes, preserving a modesty his friends were unfamiliar with. The fear of being interrupted or being shouted at by some oddball kept him to generalities and he bravely sacrificed certain more or less authentic stories he had absorbed from others and had begun to genuinely believe as true, as part of his own experience.

It's not known if he convinced any of the timid men there to enlist, but Jones' talk was certainly successful and the crowd cheered him. As he got down from the dais, he thought he heard a voice above the clapping hands shout out: "Bravo, Biscuits!"

Jones left the meeting without checking if his imagination had deceived him.

But success intoxicated him, so that he overdid his part among his circle of friends. The biscuits story became widespread without anyone knowing how and the monstrous doubt spread like an ugly, unhealthy mould.

Now he scarcely limped. His convalescent period ended at a propitious time. Jones began to have a vague idea that London had seen enough of him. He was sad and a little disgusted by the profession of arms when he got on the train at Victoria Station one morning.

"Hello, Biscuits" were the first words that welcomed him on his return to the trenches. The chant began to increase, perhaps because his comrades felt somewhat jealous of his recent long stay in London.

Things became more acrimonious one evening because Private Harry Plimmer asked him too emphatically to pass the "bloody biscuits". The men were behind at the back of the Front and had more spare time and consequently needed more to distract them. The monotony was broken that evening as soon as Jones and Plimmer faced each other, with bare arms and threatening fists. The fight did not satisfy either of them for both bore on their faces the damage made by their adversary. They were both punished by their lieutenant for having wasted their strength and energy, instead of reserving both for the fight against the Boches. The moment came more quickly than expected, although they had been waiting for it for months.

All hell from two artillery units broke loose above their heads. Then the officers of both sides went into action – one against the other – ferocious beasts that had been men. Enraged beings fighting with men's weapons, weapons of beasts and demons. For they used lead and steel, claws, teeth and strangleholds, fire and breath poisoned in former hells.

It lasted part of the night. No one really knew who was victorious. The only thing that counted was who held the ground. There were a lot of Boches and quite a lot of Tommies in khaki lying on French soil.

Corporal Jones was found seriously wounded. An ambulance took him to the nearest hospital. There, he stayed for a long time, inert without the mental or emotional energy to think. He was only aware that he was suffering and he had dreams and visions that did not involve him, that were not even part of the world he had lived in.

At last the day came when he regained consciousness. It felt like he had left the thick black mud of an abyss. He was astonished to be alive. He knew he was, because he had a heavy pain pressing on his left thigh.

Later, the nurse told him that they had amputated his leg above the knee. And the kind woman, who was so used to handle cruel, intense pain, was astonished to see the wounded man's face light up as if she had just told him some good news. He wanted to know. He was told a grenade had injured his kneecap.

Corporal Jones' eyes opened to take possession once again of life with all it held that was good, all the promises it contained. He asked for something to drink. Then he said in a voice that was still weak: "By Jove! this time, it wasn't biscuits!"

The nurse nodded in agreement and smiled, but did not understand what he meant. And Jones went back to sleep, without explaining.

Another Wenz writer

Paul Wenz's great nephew, Denis Wenz (1928-2007 – grandson of Paul's younger brother Alfred) carried on the family tradition of writing. He translated his great uncle's only book written in English *Diary of a New Chum* (1908), entitled *Un Australien tout neuf* (1989). In the translated text, Denis kept some English expressions and words as Paul had done throughout his other writings about Australia and Australians. These 'Australianisms' are in italics in the text and their explanations appear at the end of the diary.[5]

Denis retained a clear memory of his Uncle Paul when he was five: 'a very tall man who enjoyed placing a child's hand in his hand. The child's hand covered only the palm of the extended hand.'[6] Like his loved forbear, Denis wrote short stories.

After the Baccalauréat, he undertook a two-year preparatory program for an Arts Degree at the prestigious Lycée Louis Le Grand in Paris, gaining a certificate in Law. At the Sorbonne he obtained a certificate in English and Classical Literature. His grandfather's death decided him to join the family business instead of continuing his literary studies. His own father had also turned his hand to writing, with the publication of *Mon journal. Voyage autour du monde 1884-1885*, an account of his experiences travelling around the world, especially during his time in Australia – 'the wool country *par excellence*' – to gain knowledge of how to undertake business transactions when he returned to the family company.[7] So Denis followed in his father's footsteps.

"Le Thé" (Tea) originally began with an incident told to him by a friend in 1962. Then, when he and his wife Nicole took some Australian friends to the impressive and emotionally-moving war cemetery at Villers-Bretonneux, he decided: 'I definitely have to write this story'. [8] The story encapsulates two major aspects of his great uncle's life: living in Australia, running a large agricultural grazing property and overseeing his family's wool-buying agencies in Sydney and Melbourne; and the tragedy of the Great War shared between Australians and the French. In July 1938, after his last long travel holiday, Paul had participated in French-Australian ceremonies at Villers-Bretonneux.

Denis had worked for thirty-seven years in the family's wool company, which had been established by Emile Wenz at Reims in 1859. After the Great War, for practical and financial reasons, Emile decided not to return to Reims. Instead, he set up an office in Paris and opened one in London in 1919 as well. In 1923, the company expanded to Perth in Western Australia, from Melbourne and Sydney. Denis Wenz continued the traditional family wool business from 1948. And between 1950 until the business was closed in 1980, Denis became well acquainted with Australia and Australians on his many visits as a representative of the firm. His wife Nicole – whose father had been seriously wounded near Reims in September 1915 – accompanied him in 1969 and describes her experience as *'un merveilleux voyage'*.[9]

The simple, understated narrative style of "Tea" contrasts with the deep emotions that the story evokes. Denis captures the challenges people on the land have coping with the often harsh climatic conditions as well as the tragic loss of a son, their only son, who joined the thousands of Australians lying in French soil. The impact of the story requires the reader to understand the place that tea had in the culture of the Australian outback and coffee in the North of France.[10]

Tea

Denis Wenz

(with acknowledgement to Paul Wenz)

Young Tim stayed in France. Not in Paris, or on the Cote d'Azur, but somewhere between Villers-Bretonneux and Corbie in the Somme. His grave is not marked with 'known to God' although he most certainly was. Inscribed for people to see was his name, his unit and the date he died, 1917.

He had few friends in France as he had been too busy fighting. His parents, Old Tim and Mary, had been given the address of an elderly couple who young Tim had been billeted with several times when he was on leave from the Front. Monsieur and Madame Quesnoy lived in a village whose name ended in "court", not far from where Tim was on leave for the last time. In his letters home, Tim had called them Victor and Louise.

On the other side of the globe, near Cowra in New South Wales, Old Tim and Mary owned a large sheep station. They were able to run the business with a manager and other staff: maintain the fences in good condition; shear the sheep and sell the lambs. They thought of Tim when they got up in the morning and throughout the day, especially when it was time for "high tea". While this was being prepared — it was a ritual to carry the teapot to the kettle, never vice versa — it was as if young Tim was on his way back from the paddocks and would soon be sitting at the table with them. They almost never spoke about him. When they did, it was simple, almost with feigned indifference. Sorrow is an underground river in these parts, and the marks of mourning are scarcely discernible on faces tanned by the sun.

That year, there was no memorable drought or catastrophic flood. Lambing was good. Shortly after the war, the world was hungry for wool. Bails of wool with its strong characteristic odour were sold at a high price in the barking sheds of the Wool Exchange. Old Tim and Mary decided to take a trip "home" since, like everyone, they called "home" places they had never set foot on.

Once they were in England, the dangerous voyage that Tim had made to get to France (and, in the other direction, so many of his wounded mates, nurses and those accompanying them) was easy for them. They hired a car and driver and soon the village belltower where Victor and Louise lived was visible and then disappeared with each fold in the ground, as the towers in this region usually do.

The welcome was warm. A reasonable amount of conversation was possible with their driver's shaky English. The outside of the brick cottage was no indicator of the meticulous cleanliness inside. The garden resembled a page from a book of "how to" that would have shown French vegetables in their best colours. A coke stove was blazing in the main room.

Quite simply and silently, memories of young Tim came back: there was the coat-peg behind the door where he hung his digger hat; the feed bucket he willingly carried out to the animals, his rolled up sleeves ready to help with the washing up. They even gently mimicked his rudimentary French.

Knowing that the English liked this magically eccentric potion, Louise had bought some tea. She prepared it the same way she would her usual chicory coffee and the pot stayed for hours on the corner of the stove. What resulted from this method, I have never experienced. It seemed that the colour, bitter taste and strength of the liquid could make the most courageous of people recoil. Old Tim and Mary glanced momentarily at one another. Then, since the tea also tasted of appease-ment and friendship, they sipped it slowly — like nectar.

NOTES

[1] 'La Maison grise', *Bonnes gens de la Grande Guerre*, Berger-Levrault, Paris, 1919, 36-46.

[2] 'L'Aveugle et le paralytique', *Bonnes gens de la Grande Guerre*, 17-23 ; translated as 'The Incurables', in EV Lucas, *Twixt Eagle and Dove*, Methuen & Co Ltd, London, 1918, 209-14.

[3] 'Le Caporal Jones', *Bonnes gens de la Grande Guerre*, 56-63; translated as 'Biscuits', in Lucas, *Twixt Eagle and Dove*, 203-8.

[4] *Agora* was the Greek gathering place or assembly – the birthplace of democracy.

[5] Paul Wenz, *Un Australien tout neuf*, trans. by Denis Wenz, La Petite Maison, Boulogne, 1989.

[6] Email from Mme Nicole Wenz, 28 September 2017.

[7] Emile Wenz, *Mon journal. Voyage autour du monde 1884-1885*, E Plon, Nourrit et Cie, Paris, 1886.

[8] 'Il faut absolument que j'écrive cette nouvelle', email, 22 September 2017.

[9] Mme Nicole Wenz to Marie Ramsland, Meudon, 9 avril, 7 mai and 14 juin 2013.

[10] Nicole Wenz to Marie Ramsland, 13 août 2013: 'Il fallait connaître l'importance de ces "rites", le THÉ, pour vous, le CAFÉ dans le Nord de la France (souvent mêlé de CHICORÉE, pour en saisir le sens !'

ACKNOWLEDGEMENTS

My sincere thanks to Dr Jean-Paul Delamotte AM for sending me a copy of *Le Pays de leurs pères* along with encouragement for my translation. His generosity and continued support have been invaluable.

I thank him also for putting me in contact with Mme Nicole Wenz. She sent me copies of the two volumes of war stories Paul had written, a collective publication about Protestants in Reims and postcards depicting the bombing of Reims during the Great War, her husband Denis' recently-published writings and a selection of family photographs. I deeply appreciate the time and effort she took to provide me with relevant information by email and letter.

The Wenz collection of books and archival material, including photographs, held in the Mitchell Library, and the assistance of the NSW State Library staff provided a rich source of information for the Introduction. The Auchmuty Library of the University of Newcastle also holds many of the recent publications of Wenz's writings.

For encouragement and support given to me by my husband John in this endeavour, I am grateful. His knowledge of Australian military and cultural history, at times, assisted my choice of words and expressions. The cover image – "Mustering Sheep" by W Hatherell, *Sydney Mail* (1917) – was an image he found.

Working with ETT Imprint has been a pleasure. The professional support of director Tom Thompson and his staff has enabled the process of publishing to flow smoothly. For this I am deeply appreciative.

PUBLICATIONS

Published by La Petite Maison, Boulogne-Billancourt

En époussetant la Mappemonde (souvenirs inédits), 2009

Le Trader, 2005

Récits du bush: trois nouvelles australiennes, containing 'Picky',
'Le Petit Murphy' and 'Le Cockatoo', 1998

Le Pays de leurs pères: suivi de letteres retrouvées de l'auteur et
  d'André Gide, 1996.

Paul Wenz (1869-1939): sa vie son oeuvre, 1998.

L'Homme du Soleil Couchant: suivi des lettres à Joseph Krug, 1993.

Un Australien tout neuf (1908) 1989, translated by
  Denis Wenz.

L 'Echarde: avant-propos d'André Gide, 1988.

Published by ETT Imprint, Exile Bay

The Thorn in the Flesh, translated by Maurice Blackman, 2004, 2018.

Diary of a New Chum, 1990.